She Spoke in Tongues

Glory Sasikala Franklin

Setu Publications

PITTSBURGH, USA

She Spoke in Tongues
By

Glory Sasikala Franklin

Setu Publications
* Pittsburgh, PA (USA) *

© 2018 by Glory Sasikala Franklin

We would be pleased to receive email correspondence regarding this publication or related topics at setuedit@gmail.com.

ISBN-13 (paperback): 978-1-947403-06-2
Cover Design by Anurag Sharma
Cover Image courtesy https://pixabay.com/
Printed and bound in the United States of America.
Distributed to the book trade worldwide by Setu Publications, Pittsburgh (USA)

Setu Literary Publications, Pittsburgh, USA

She Spoke in Tongues

Glory Sasikala Franklin

Dedication

I dedicate this book to my father, C.A. Pillay, for recognizing something special in a 7-year-old, enough to encourage her all that he could, knowing he had very little time left. Time ran out three years later. Time has stood still in a lot of ways since that fateful day when I watched them nail his coffin, but he has lived through me all these years, and every time I pick up my pen, I say, "Daddy, this is for you."

Acknowledgements

I thank the editors and publishers of the *Setu* where 'She Spoke in Tongues' first appeared as a serial.

Special Mentions

My mother, Late Smt. Seshammal Pillay
My husband, Late P. Vijayakumar Franklin
My sister, Mary Rajalakshmi
My brother, Anand Kumar Pillay
My son, V. Tennyson
My daughter, V. Rimona
My daughter-in-law, Hannah
and last but not least,
My grandson, Baby Samuel.

And a BIG THANK YOU to all my well-wishers and every single one of you who has read and appreciated the story and is eager to buy the book. It's readers like you that keep me going.

Lots of Love and Best Wishes,

GLORY SASIKALA

Contents

'She Spoke In Tongues' is my first foray into writing for adults. It's not my first published novel. My first novel—or rather novelette—is 'Goodbye Papa,' published by Prof. P. Lal, Writers Workshop, Kolkata, written about the rights and dignity of children. It's been more than two decades since I wrote that. A lot has happened since then, and my life has changed drastically. My husband died in a tragic road accident in 2008. I had to fend for my family and provide for my two children, which kept me occupied and on my toes. But the dream was, has been, and will always be to write. The children have grown up and I am finally able to pick up my pen again and find the peace and quiet so necessary to create. I was absolutely thrilled when Sunil Sharma and Anurag Sharma from Setu Mag graciously agreed to allow me to not only serialize my second novel in the magazine but also to go ahead and publish it as a book. My humble thanks and gratitude to them.

That's when I faced my second dilemma (lack of time being the first one). I was not comfortable with writing for adults, by which, I guess I mean that I was not comfortable with sexual content. My strict upbringing would not allow me to talk about subjects that my mother considered 'taboo'. And yet, I felt incomplete as a writer because I felt writers should be able transcend all barriers and be true to their storytelling. With age, and with more exposure to the world, I had become more relaxed in my attitude. I was also able to express myself better, if only when amongst close friends. So, as a step towards breaking this self-inflicted barrier, I decided to deliberately go in for a bolder plot. After exploring all the information at my disposal—the heard, the said, and the experienced, I was finally able to string together a storyline. I chose to feature refugees because I do know some bit about their ways and their struggles. My father was originally from Burma (the current Myanmar) and had walked to India along with his sisters and father during the World War after his house was bombed. I have observed closely refugees from Bangladesh when we lived in Kolkata, and refugees from Sri Lanka after we shifted to South India. I have to reiterate here that this is, however, not the story of all immigrants or refugees but rather specific to this one particular family and their struggles for survival in a strange and alien land. It is also not even remotely connected to my father's life or his family, and it is definitely not the story of any real-life family.

Crimes against children disturb me more than any other. And when I read of real-life stories where mothers sell their daughters—some as young as 5 years old—I find it hard to comprehend. How can one's own mother do that? What do they tell themselves, what is their internal dialogue that tells them that it's okay? What kind of women would do that? What kind of mothers would do that? Most of the time, the reason is poverty, and sometimes, as is the case in this book, it is greed. I've tried to explore the thought process both for myself and for my readers, the crossing over to the ruthless by these mothers who sell their daughters. It was painful writing, and it makes painful reading. Stories must be told, and I hope that this story will bring into focus the fact that these tragic events happen in every society, and I hope that it can be addressed. I hope poverty can be eradicated, which, in turn, will eradicate child prostitution.

These are high hopes indeed, but every little step in the right direction helps. The book also addresses other issues, such as the strong hold that the caste system still has over the Indian society, despite innumerous measures to eradicate it.

Eventually, the book is a triumph of righteousness over wrong living. It deals with the consequences of living the wrong way versus those living the right way. The right path is arduous, less travelled, but the very decision to stay with it brings peace, goodwill, and happiness. Wrong living can never lead to happiness.

I hope that you, my readers, enjoy reading this story, gripping as it is, and I hope that you run through a gambit of emotions, ranging from sympathy to anger to horror, following this much-flawed family's journey. If the story touches you in any way, if you feel like letting me know your thoughts and opinions, do write in to me at glorysasikala@gmail.com. I will be waiting to hear from you.

Love and Best Wishes,

Glory Sasikala Franklin

CHAPTER 1

for you to resolve your maybes and maybe nots
I could not wait
There was never a good time, and when there was
It was too late

She looked into the distance with seeking, craving eyes. East! Burma was East! How far they had come! They had walked for days and nights on end, over the North Eastern mountains, the Himalayas, and reached Calcutta. What day was it, what month? It must be going two months and more now, and they were still on the move. Being South Indians, they had been put on the train to Madras. What beheld them when they reached Madras? A new life...hopefully a secure one. She watched as the Howrah Bridge appeared, the Hoogly slowly and leisurely winding its way to the ocean, the boats gently floating, dancing to the rhythm of gentle waves, a glorious scene of receding Sunset twilight.

But she was far away in her thoughts, in another country, another time.

British colonization of Burma had somehow been inclusive, and the country stretched in a panoramic view, still a secluded sylvan haven of blue hills, green meadows, tropical forests, and, of course, the winding, blue zigzagging line of the Irrawaddy River that cut through lush plains in a sure course to the ocean. Farmers tilled the land in the hot Sun, revelling in the abundance of water supply and the promise of a rich harvest. Time was still an abundant resource, even as inhabitants went about their dailies. There was time to listen to a bird call, stay with the radio till a song was over, serenade a maiden till she was ready to say yes, take a dog out for a walk over the fields, and wrap up the day with a glass of beer in the company of friends. And there still was time for families to celebrate togetherness.

The day drew to its conclusion, and the little mites who had troubled the farmer by climbing over the stile to milk the cow, taken pot shots with a catapult at the chameleon on the fence, introduced mice in the classroom, played football in the rain, and swung down the branches of the old banyan tree to drop pell-mell into the flowing Irrawaddy river, were all now asleep, their faces in repose the very picture of innocence.

But in their heart of hearts, everyone knew that this time was precious, an interlude, because there was war and strife all over the world. World War II was on. Which side were they on? This, no one knew. They just knew that they were the perfect target, Burma being situated as it was, cocooned between India and China. Sometimes...no, nowadays, frequently, they all looked up at the sky, at the far horizon, for the dreaded sound of planes, of dropping bombs. It seemed so unbelievable that it could happen. Look at the Earth, so quiet! So peaceful! So sylvan! And yet...

Had they but known!

The night progressed, and soon it was that time before daybreak. Rosy twilight spread over the gardens, gaining ground over the darkness, and then on to the spacious bedroom, making the world a very pink place indeed. He stirred in his sleep and moved a hand to cover his eyes. He then opened his eyes tentatively and peered through his fingers. Not finding the twilight intrusive, he removed his hand and sighed deeply. Birds chirped gustily outside, each one with its very own special morning song, heralding in the new day. He turned to look at her, lying there on her back, a little away from him. The view was delectable, as always. His wife was so very beautiful! Even in sleep, her features seemed sculpted. And then too, she was a courtesan! Yes, he had married a courtesan. Unbelievable! But there it was!

Life after marriage had been wonderful. He could not get enough of her, or she of him. But she was a courtesan alright. Making love, wooing, knowing what turned on a man, it all came naturally to her. By birth a courtesan...

Tharani's mother had been extremely beautiful and talented. She could sing beautifully and dance well too. She had never been short of wooers. Well-connected and wealthy men courted her and showered her with money and gifts. Tharani had grown up in the lap of luxury. She had had everything a girl could wish for... except respectability. She watched men walk in and out of her mother's life. Most of them were good to her, but as Tharani grew up, she understood what her mother did for a living, and it made her sad. Men walked in and out of her life, men who were kind to her. The men had been fatherly when she was a child, but as she grew up and became more beautiful by the day, their attention turned from her mother on to herself and became sexual in nature. Her mother watched the transition sadly. She was old now and alone. She knew no other means to sustain them. And then, one day, when she was 16, Tharani had woken up and walked over to her mother's room and found her dead. She had died in her sleep. That was the turning point in Tharani's young life. She had decided to take over where her mother had left off and be a courtesan too. Not a cheap prostitute but an escort who worked exclusively and stayed with one wealthy man at a time for as long as he wanted her to be there.

Tharani understood only too well how it all worked. She was a natural. Playing up to men, understanding their needs, it all came to her naturally. She was only 18 and two years into it when Sushanth walked into her life...and everything changed. She had gone with her mentor to Sushanth's office during one of his business trips. Sushanth and his partner, Vineeth, ran a law firm in the heart of the city. Her mentor was a wealthy old man in his fifties. He was a widower and he enjoyed her company, young and beautiful as she was. He had asked her to wait in the car while he wrapped up some business. But she found that he had left his spectacles behind. She took these and went into the office. Sushanth had looked up from his desk and they had instantly fallen in love with each other. The rest, as they say, was history.

Sushanth's parents had died when he was a two-year-old baby. He had been brought up his maternal uncle and aunt. They had four children of their own and another addition to the family had not made much of a difference to them. They welcomed him wholeheartedly into their fold. His childhood had been a happy one. At the time when had Sushanth turned 21, his uncle had decided to return to India with his family and settle there, feeling it was a safer option under the volatile and uncertain circumstances. Sushanth had opted to stay back as he had his own law firm now that he ran with his partner, Vineeth. So, when he decided to marry Tharani, there was no one to oppose the decision in any way. His friends were concerned, yes, but when they saw how determined he was, they shrugged and accepted the inevitable.

Vineeth was Sushanth's partner and best friend. His wife, Shanthi, was Tharani's good friend. The two families lived in the same building, their houses separated only by a landing. Vineeth and Shanthi had two children of their own—twin girls about 10 years old. The children ran freely into each other's house.

Having never been part of a normal family, Tharani valued her 'respectable' status a lot. She liked to talk to Shanthi as 'we,' meaning 'we respectable people'. "We don't do such things," she would say. Shanthi, who knew all about Tharani's shady past, was sensitive enough not to make fun of her or be sarcastic. She loved Tharani and had her best interests at heart. Tharani also had a love for people from the 'upper caste' and liked associating with them. She had no clue what caste she belonged to. She knew Sushanth was from an upper caste, and she liked him all the more for it. She would go to the temple and seek out these women and try to befriend them. Her 'we people' comments never went well with them and quite some snide remarks were passed about her background when she was not present.

Sushanth and Tharani now had three children, three lovely little girls. Their whole world centred on their children. Tharani now spent all her time being a good mother, completely engrossed in her family. She was a wonderful cook and had a real talent for housekeeping. She could make the tiniest of spaces look fantastic. She was also an excellent tailor. She stitched all her clothes and her children's clothes too.

Life couldn't be better, thought Sushanth.

He turned to his side and lifted himself on his elbow for a better perspective. "How beautiful!" he thought for the millionth time. Winged eyebrows complemented only too perfectly by the long eyelashes of the downcast eyes; the just-about-right nose with the tiniest of diamonds in the left nostril. He watched as the diamond caught the morning sunlight and twinkled. Those luscious lips! How many times he had kissed them, and yet, they remained as sensuously inviting and full, seemingly unsullied and untouched. His eyes went to her well-rounded chin. When she smiled, those enticing dimples would magically appear and he really had to kiss each one of them. He traced the contour of her chin with his forefinger, then let it run over her lips, outlining them. She stirred in her sleep and frowned. He moved his finger away, but she opened her eyes, so tawny and gold. "Go away!"

He smiled, "Good morning!"

"It's not morning yet. Turn to the other side and go to sleep."

She tried to move him away, but his arm went round her and pulled her close.

"Why do you wake me up so soon? Long day ahead… Must sleep while I can…"

"Help you sleep?"

"No!"

"Yes?"

"It's no. And no means no."

He placed a hand over her breast. "Your body says 'yes'.

"My body lies," she mumbled against his chest.

"Your eyes say it too."

"My eyes, ears, nose, body, mind, soul, spirit, they all lie!"

"Ah! So who are you?"

"I'm the one who wants to go to sleep, stupid."

"And who is it that's moving closer to me now?"

"That's ole desire. Has nothing to do with me, I assure you. I still don't want…"

He pushed her away. "If you really want to go to sleep so much, go ahead. I won't disturb you."

"Hey, don't do that! Don't push! What's wrong with you?" she asked, moving closer now. "Don't you want me?"

He rubbed his nose with his left hand and then lifted his right hand and pushed his hair back. She grinned.

"Why are you smiling?"

"Nothing," she said. The gesture was so familiar! He always did that when he was lying.

She moved closer to him and placed her head on the crook of his arm. She placed her hand his chest. "Hmmm… I guess I'll go to sleep."

"Not like this! Tharani, it's not fair."

"Everything is fair in…" but she got not further, as he pushed her down violently and claimed her lips with his own.

Outside, a little bird chirped severely, "Mind how you do it, do it!"

Bang! Bang! Bang!

"Mummy! Are you there? Open the door!"

Bang!

A smaller voice called, "Daddy!"

Sushanth and Tharani hurriedly separated and looked towards the door. Then they turned towards each other and smiled.

"We'd better be quick. They're quite likely to break open the door."

They hurriedly got dressed, then Sushanth opened the door.

"What took you so long?" Sitara demanded. She was their second child, now 10 years old. "Do you know how long we've been standing here?"

"Sorry!" said Sushanth, holding his ears.

"Have you two been kissing?"

"Hmm...sort of."

Sitara looked disgusted. Then she shrugged as she came into the room, "I don't care anyways. It's annual day. Yey!!!"

"Yey!!" said little five-year-old Sheila. She had, meanwhile, clambered up the bed and was now too safely and snugly settled in her mother's arms to bother much about anything else. She plastered her mother's face with kisses and looked up at her adoringly. "I love you!"

"I do too, darling!" said Tharani, meaning every word of it. She kissed her baby girl too. "You're the best Mummy in the whole world!"

"And you're the best baby in the whole world!"

Sitara snorted from where she stood by the bed, "Don't pet her too much. She peed in her bed. I changed her clothes."

And before her mother could reply, she turned impatiently to her father, "When are you coming to school?"

"Any time you want me to," he replied with a sly smile.

"But... aren't you going to work?"

He settled back on a pillow, "Um...I'm thinking not today. I'm thinking I'll take leave."

"Daddy!" she screamed and jumped right into his arms. "You're the best!"

"Is that so?" he laughed.

"Yes, Daddy!" She put her palms on both sides of his face to direct his attention completely towards her, a warning for her father that she was going to make a fairly impossible request.

"Daddy, will you buy me this biology box."

"What's that?"

"It's what the older students use for biology. For dissecting and stuff. It's got all sorts of things in it, like scissors and knives. It's also got a magnifying glass, Daddy."

"Hmmm… why would you want that?"

She looked surprised, "For dissecting. What else would I want it for? I'm going to be a naturalist when I grow up. I need to collect insects and plants and things, and I need to dissect things."

"I thought you were going to be an Airforce pilot?"

"Yes, that too! A lady pilot, imagine!" her beautiful tawny gold eyes gleamed. "I can be both."

Sushanth smiled at this tomboy girl. "You're ambitious."

She sighed, "Yes…there're so many interesting things to do. Daddy, will you get me the box?"

"We'll see."

Tharani, who was listening in on the conversation said sarcastically, "Yes, spoil her some more. As if she's not enough trouble already. Her teacher is complaining that she threw Rashmi's eraser out of the window. Why should a girl get so angry?"

"Mum, she ate my lunch!"

"Thank God someone ate it. I'm fed up of throwing food out daily. Anyways, you buy her that box, the house is going to be full of all sorts of insects. Even snakes, maybe. Who knows what goes on in her head?"

"Momze! You keep out of this okay? This doesn't concern you."

She turned to her father, "Daddy, please don't listen to her. She's always complaining about me."

"We'll see," repeated Sushanth, pulling her hair.

She put her hand to her head, "My favourite curl is gone!"

And all her doting father could see was there were enough adorable curls all over her head and cascading down her shoulders.

"You have so many curls!"

"I'll give you the second best curl if you get me the box."

Sushanth turned to his wife, "Now, tell me, how do I say no to that?"

Tharani snorted, "Both father and daughter are not okay," she said conversationally to Sheila.

"Mummy! You take that back!" said Sitara, "Say we're good people."

"No ways!" challenged Tharani, looking defiantly at this daughter of hers so very like her, both in looks and character. The same unruly curls, the same tawny gold eyes and dusky, glowing complexion, and the same fearless fighting spirit. The lioness and her cub.

"I'll make you!" said Sitara, jumping on to her mother's side of the bed and on to her.

Sushanth got off the bed and lifted Sheila. "Come on, let's go. They're going to kill each other. We don't want to be witnesses."

"But I don't want Mummy to die!"

"Don't worry, darling. I'll get you another mother."

"Sushanth!" screamed Tharani, "How dare you!"

He chuckled and left the room with Sheila, calling back, "I'm switching on the geyser. Make breakfast if you're still alive."

He walked out and entered the other room. A lone figure was seated at the centre of the room, a young 13-year-old girl, Yamini, his eldest. She was a quiet child, studious and inclined to take life too seriously. Hers was a rare beauty, one that was not immediately recognizable. You had to look at her closely, take in the features of her face one by one, to realize that she was indeed extremely beautiful. Her hair was long and done in plaits.

She looked despondent as she sat there, staring at the floor.

"Yamini?"

"Yes Daddy?"

"What's the matter, child?"

"Daddy, will I be able to speak well today?"

She was to do the Welcome Address at the Annual Day function at their school.

"Yes, of course! That's why they've chosen you. They wouldn't if they thought you wouldn't be able to do it. So many children, and yet they chose you. That should tell you something."

She looked at him with hopeful eyes then, "Yes... yes, you're right. I will do well."

She smiled cheerfully then. "There!" said Sushanth. "Go and practice a few times more. The more you practice, the more comfortable you'll be."

"Okay Daddy."

And it was at that very moment that the first boom sounded.

It sounded like it was coming from far. But after a short interval, a second boom sounded. This time too, it was distant. Vineeth was knocking frantically on the door. "Sushanth, open the door!" Bang! Bang! Bang!

Sushanth hurried to open the door. "Run for your lives, all of you! They're bombing the place. Run! Hurry up!" and then, Vineeth pushed Shanthi in front of him and started running. When Sushanth looked out the gate, they were both gone!

It took a moment for what Vineeth had said to register, and then he jumped into action. He grabbed Sheila's hand, he pushed Yamini and Sitara in front of him and screamed, "Run! Run both of you!" They looked back at him, uncertain and hesitating. He screamed again, "Just run!" He turned and shouted, "Tharani, drop everything you're doing and run!" Tharani was already out there. She heard him. She went in to switch off the gas. "Leave everything and run!" And Sushanth ran out of the house, holding Sheila's hand. Tharani ran behind him, but he was soon out of the gate. She stopped, and went back into the house. She picked up a bag, opened the wardrobe and emptied her gold jewels into it. She then stuffed a couple of saris over them. She then ran out, but hesitated once more. Vineeth's house was open. She went in, and to the bedroom. The wardrobe was not locked. She opened it, emptied the jewels into her bag. Then she ran out of the gate, and as fast as she could. When she reached the end of the road, she turned to look back at their house... just in time to see a bomb flying down over it. BOOM!!

And then it all went grey.

someone tapped me gently, from my dreams to arouse
who is it, I wondered. 'Twas the Moon above my house

"Pass me the salt."

"Sitara, sit straight."

"You never tell her to sit straight!"

"Sheila, sit straight."

"You're just saying that to appease me."

"Appease? Who taught you such big words? We don't need to appease you anyways. You have to do what you're told."

"Mummy, I won't…"

"Yamini, please bring in the ladle. I forgot."

"I don't want cauliflower."

"Mix it with the rice. Here let me show you."

The conversation went on around the table at dinner. The family had settled down in Madras very nicely indeed. With almost nothing to get them going, no assets or papers, except, of course, the jewels that Tharani had so wisely—or unwisely—taken with her, they had managed to come a long, long way. Tharani had given Shanthi her jewels, and Shanthi had been ever so grateful. The two families kept in touch with each other. Indeed, in this strange country, all the immigrants from Burma kept in touch and helped each other out. They met regularly, celebrated festivals together, took their children out together, had parties. Not that there was much to celebrate, and certainly not enough money to go around.

Both Vineeth and Sushanth had rented houses in the same area, Sowkarpet, so famous for the wholesale markets. Rickshaws still plied here, trams were still on the roads. Each street boasted a wholesale: wholesale of steel utensils, wholesale of bags, wholesale of wedding items, wholesale of sarees. And, a little further away, in a little outer circle that was quieter, and besides a common, on Mulla Street, Sushanth has found a nice house for his family. He now did electrical work and ran a shop. Tharani had started a tailoring unit in the house itself. She was very good with the needle and she had quite a clientele. She was the one tailor who knew how to stitch that elusive perfect blouse that had no creases around the armpit area. She flexed easily with her customers' needs, understood them perfectly, made no judgement calls, and delivered on time. Her fame spread by word of mouth and her customers nodded their heads wisely and said, "She is from Burma. These foreigners have magic in their fingers. There is no equalling their talents."

Two years had passed by. The children were older. They now had sufficient money, enough anyhow to send two children to school. Sitara and Sheila went to a good school nearby. But they could not afford to send Yamini. She had to work too to add to their income, at least till they were well settled. Two streets away lived a small family, a mother, father and two toddlers aged 4 and 2. There was also a very old grandmother. The mother needed someone to help her out while she coped with her family's demands, and Yamini fitted the bill perfectly. She left for work at around 9.30 am in the morning and returned back home in the evening by 6 pm. She did everything that she was told. Her jobs included running errands, taking care of the babies, helping around the kitchen and helping take care of and bathing the Grandma. Very arduous days they were for her, and she was very tired in the evening. But she was a good girl and very understanding. She understood that her family was not as they were before, that money was scarce, that her parents were struggling to make ends meet. As the eldest child, she felt it was her duty to share their burdens, to see that the younger two got a good education. If only she did not like studying so much! If only she did not look at the books with so much longing! Even then, things weren't that bad. She read Sitara's school books and kept herself updated. Her employer, Anita, was a good woman too. She allowed Yamini to borrow some of her books so long as they were returned back in good condition.

Dinner was over and everything was cleared up. The table was cleared and cleaned, and the two younger ones sat down to study and do their homework. For Yamini, this was the best part of the day. She sat eagerly next to Sitara, picking up the books, reading, hearing stories about their school life.

Tharani washed the dishes, cleaned up the kitchen, made some tea and poured it in two cups and placed the cups in a tray, and moved out of the kitchen and out into the porch, where Sushanth stood by the gate, and from the darkness of the porch, he could see into the house to where the girls sat around the table. He was gazing intently at them and his eyes glistened with unshed tears. Tharani looked at him and knew what he was thinking. "She will do well for now," she said gently, "Very understanding child."

"Yes….yes. Of course."

Tharani looked at him as she handed him his teacup. "What are you thinking?"

"I'm thinking she should be in school. The one child who was born to study."

"We'll send her."

"When?" he said, and there was frustration in his voice.

Tharani's eyes widened.

"When we can afford it. We've started earning quite well now. A few more days…"

"It won't happen."

"Why are you talking like that? You've lost hope so soon."

"Don't you see? We've reached stagnation. This is how far my business will go. This is how far yours will too. The same clients, the same demands…saturation. We need to think and do something else, something different."

"Sounds nice. Pertinent question: like what?"

Sushanth looked at her then for a moment, then he turned abruptly towards the gate. In that one moment that she held his gaze, Tharani saw something that sent a shiver down her spine. He was onto something, and that something wasn't good!

But she waited; she stayed quiet and drank her tea. "Something…" she heard him whisper into the night.

Her hand stilled as her cup hovered near her mouth. She put down her cup and went to him and placed a hand over his shoulder. "Sushanth, what is it?"

He looked at her again for her moment but could not meet her eye. She turned him to face her. "Sushanth, what is it? Whatever it is, you can tell me."

He looked at her then and saw the fear in her eyes, the tiny trickle of sweat at her temple. His eyes softened. "It's nothing. Just…. Nothing really."

She continued to look at him. He sighed, "You won't let go, will you?"

"No."

"Well, you might as well know. Vineeth is leaving for Bombay."

Her eyes widened at that. "Why?"

Sushanth shrugged. "He...wants to open a store there. A supermarket."

"But... where did he get the money?"

"That..." He was literally squirming now, "Look, can you just let this be?"

"No! Tell me! What is it?"

"Well, Shanthi..."

"Shanthi?"

"Well, you know that old doctor man who runs the Pandey Clinic?"

"Dr. Vidyasagar Pandey?"

"Yes."

"Well, he and Shanthi..."

Tharani's eyes widened, "You mean...?"

Prashanth shrugged expressively.

"But the man is so old!"

"And lonely?"

"Yes...lonely....." Tharani's voice trailed off as a new thought struck her, the one he was dreading.

"Sushanth, you don't think I should...?"

"No, of course not silly!"

"But the thought occurred to you!"

"No, it did not!" He rubbed his hand vigorously over his nose.

She looked at him then, "Sushanth, you only rub your nose when you're lying.

"Damn!"

He took her hands, "Look, I'm sorry. Yes, the thought occurred in my depraved mind, but it's gone, see? It won't happen again."

Tharani wasn't listening to him. She was looking inside the house to where the girls sat. Yamini was discussing something animatedly with Sitara and showing her something in her book.

"She must study."

"Tharani!"

Tharani looked up at him, and Sushanth knew she had made up her mind. "She will study."

The stars looked down at them then, like old sages, and the Moon walked past the stars, sweeping her skirts over them as she did, and she said disdainfully, "Humans beings are so greedy!"

CHAPTER 3

Think of me and I'll be present
full and bright or just a crescent

When catastrophe strikes and the carpet is slipped from underneath your feet in one single moment, and life as you knew it is gone forever, it's hard to feel secure again, trust again. The 'what ifs' prevail. What if it happens again? One feels the need to anchor somewhere, and that anchor most of the time, is belief in a higher power, one that will be there and protect you and see you through it all.

Sitara and Sheila had left for school and Yamini and Sushanth for work, and Tharani was alone at home. Tuesdays were half-day off from her tailoring as she always visited the temple. She had her bath and donned a crisp cotton sari. Her hair was wet and she left it open. She never wore slippers to the temple. It was a kind of penance, and it always pertained to the fulfilment of some particular prayer. She picked up her basket of flowers and fruits and coconuts—her offerings to God—and left for the temple.

She prayed, and then, circled the temple thirteen times. Tired out, she sat down on the steps to the pool. It felt very peaceful to just sit there and rest and feel the cool breeze. Temples were a respite to so many tired and seeking souls. An added advantage was that they were always open and welcoming. For women, going to the temple was also a time to socialize. They sometimes came in groups and exchanged news and enjoyed each other's company. One such group of three women now sat quite close to Tharani, just behind her and she could hear their rather heart-to-heart and open conversation, without actually eavesdropping.

"I got my chums. Again," said a young woman. "I don't think I'm ever going to conceive."

"You're doing it right?" asked another, mischievously.

"Of course we're doing it right. We know the right way." All of them were laughing now.

"I shouldn't be laughing," said the young woman who could not conceive, "I think my husband is not interested in me."

There was an awkward silence. Then one of the other women said, "Why do you think so? Don't you…?"

"We do. Once in a while...once or twice a month. He's not there emotionally. It's all so...perfunctory now."

The other woman said, "Happens all the time. Work pressure. And, with time, it does become kind of mechanical."

"It's not that. I feel... I'm sorry, but I feel he's seeing someone else."

Silence again.

Then one of the other women said, "Would you be willing to take some risks—I mean real risks—to get him back?"

"Anything! I would be willing to do anything! Why? Can you help me?"

"Well, they say there's this Forest Spirit. It... she... something... lives in the forests of Kauri Hills. It comes on the way to Yercaud, some three hours from here. A lot of trains go that way, and most of them stop at this station for only two minutes. You've got to be fast getting in and out of the train. Also, I think there are no houses there—just these hills. They say they're so high, they could be mountains."

"How many trains go that way?"

"Quite a few of them. One or two local ones too."

"And?"

"And, well, you go up to the foot of the hills, and a little further."

"It sounds scary. Are there people there?"

"No. It's very risky. Anything can happen."

"Oh..."

"Anyway, you have to take some gifts. The Forest Spirit likes food—cooked vegetarian food. Don't use garlic or onions or ginger. Don't take uncooked food. Don't take the food in vessels. Use banana leaves and tie it with thread. Don't use rubber bands."

"Okay?"

"You must also wear a bright yellow sari with a green blouse and leave your hair open."

"Why is that?"

"I don't know, but that's what they say. Maybe to look like a tree with yellow flowers or something."

All of them laughed.

"Who told you that?"

"It's folklore in my village."

"Do you know anyone who's gone there?"

"One of my neighbours in my village got her daughter to go because she wasn't getting pregnant. It's an aphrodisiac made out of choice leaves, fruits, twigs, and other stuff. The Forest Spirit gets it for you."

"And?"

"She conceived in a couple of months. It was a miracle."

Silence…

"Do you want to go?"

"I don't know. What else should be done?"

"You must go barefoot."

"But that's hillside! Full of stones and thorns besides being so very hot!"

"You'll have to bear it."

"Okay. So then?"

"So then, you draw a circle around yourself with stones for protection. Then you place the food outside the circle, and then you wait."

"How will the Spirit know I'm there?"

"That's the strange part. It always does. It always comes. It's like it can smell humans."

"Brrrr! It all sounds very creepy. I'm not sure I care for my husband all that much."

The women went into peals of laughter, and Tharani was smiling too. She listened some more.

"Well, you're the one to decide."

"Can I take someone with me?"

"Apparently not. And you can't tell anyone where you're going either."

"You're purposely making this very difficult, aren't you?"

"No re, I'm not! This is how it is. The Spirit has different concoctions for different things, for infertility, for diseases, and even for purposes. Like if you want to rob a bank, there's leaves and twigs for that too."

"You're kidding me!"

"Well, yes, I couldn't help doing that," said the narrator, sounding guilty, "But the rest is true. The Spirit can read your mind."

"What language does it speak?"

"Some forest language, I guess. But its gestures are very clear."

"How does it look?"

"Strange looking, I heard. It's a woman alright, but one like you've never seen before."

The conversation continued, but Tharani felt she had heard enough. She got up to her feet, picked up her empty basket and walked back home, deep in thought.

****

Tharani was up before dawn the following Saturday. She had bought all the ingredients the previous day and finished the cutting and grinding, and now she set about preparing a complete meal. She made rice, sambar, rasam, some other hot curries, some mixed vegetable side dishes, and some cutlets. She was an excellent cook, but it had turned out to be quite a challenge to prepare dishes devoid of ginger, garlic, and onions, Indian food being all about spice and tangy flavours. But, well, it was all done and tasted very good. She carefully packed it all in banana leaves by placing the leaves on newspapers. She then folded each leaf carefully and tied it with twines. She then placed all the food in a big cloth bag. She paused for a while, wondering if there was anything else that needed to be done. Then she brought out another big cloth bag, folded it, and placed it on top of the food. After all, that was the purpose of the visit. If she was going to be given something by the Forest Spirit, she would need a bag to bring it back in.

All done in the kitchen, she neatly arranged the food for the children on the dining table. She had, of course, cooked for them as well. Sushanth wasn't there. He had left for Bombay with Vineeth the night before to help him set up his business, and hopefully, if all went well, join as partner later on. "If all went well" depended on her and the Forest Spirit. He would be back the week after. Tharani then cleaned the kitchen, washed the dishes, and then made herself a hot cup of coffee. She moved to the hall and sat there in the porch, watching daybreak. She then washed up the cup, had a bath, and donned a yellow sari with a green blouse. Her hair was wet, and she left it open. It was now just about half-past six. She then picked up the bag, went over to Yamini and shook her awake. Yamini opened her eyes and looked sleepily at her mother. "Yamini, please close and lock the door. Come!" She had explained to Yamini that she had some work the next day involving the temple and offering prayers. Yamini hadn't asked any questions. She was her mother's biggest ally, never questioning anything she said or did, but lending complete support.

They moved to the hall, and Tharani went out and Yamini closed and locked the door. Just as she was moving away, a voice called out from the porch, "Maaaaa!! Where are you going?" It was Sitara.

Tharani looked back in despair. She waved at her to go in. "I'll come and tell you. Go inside! Listen to your sister."

None of which registered in the little girl's mind. "I'm hungry!" she now shouted.

"Food is there on the table. Eat the food and stay inside."

"I'm going out," said Sitara, "To play cricket."

Tharani stopped in her tracks and looked at this defiant daughter of hers in despair. "Okay but be careful and be back home by afternoon. Don't go out after that."

"When will you be back?"

"I don't know. It will be quite late."

"Why are you dressed like that? And where are your slippers? Are you going to the temple?"

Tharani felt like going back in and smacking the little girl. "You go in and stop shouting. Please obey Sitara!"

"Okay. Please buy me something to eat."

"Okay," said Tharani, "I will. Take care of Sheila," she added cunningly, because Sitara, for all her tomboyish ways, or maybe because of them, was very protective of Sheila. "See that she doesn't get into mischief."

"Okay," said the redoubtable Sitara, and withdrew from the porch.

Tharani made her way to the railway station, bought her ticket and made her way to the day train that would be going to Yercaud. She had made her enquiries and knew that this train would stop at Kauri Hills for two minutes. She got into the last carriage in the hopes of getting down and letting the train pass by without being noticed too much. She sat down near a window and looked out. The train started to move, and she was on her way! She was supposed to get down at the Kauri Hills Station some three hour later. She kept a keen look out. About two hours and forty-five minutes into the ride, she got up and made her way to the door and stood there, waiting. Everyone else was seated, and they looked curiously at her as she stood there, but no one said anything. In India, people accepted these strange appearances and behaviour. It was obviously some form of worship and they understood that. Gradually, almost imperceptibly, the train slowed down and moved into what seemed to be a valley, with hills looming almost immediately from the tracks on both sides. Tharani looked with alarm to both right and left. The hills were very high and towering; they were the Ghats. She peeped out the door and saw a tiny station. Kauri Hills. The train slowed down and stopped and she got down. Almost immediately, the train picked up speed and was gone. She stood, looking around the station. It was nothing more than a platform really, with a room at one end, apparently for the station master. A lady stood there with a green and red flag in her hand. Tharani smiled at her, but the lady did not smile back. She looked curiously at Tharani, and then she came over. She was a pleasantly plump, middle-aged lady with squiggly hair done in a plait. One leg was shorter than the other and she limped. However, there was an air of confidence and command about her that belied this rather drab appearance. She was obviously a railway employee.

"You're here to see the Forest Spirit?"

"Yes," said Tharani, apprehensively, "Is it true?"

"You don't believe?" asked the lady.

Tharani shook her head. "I don't know. I've heard."

"It's true," the lady, nodding, "You have to go there!" She pointed to the hill on the side of the station, outside it. It was so strange to see a hill start right outside the station. "Go a little further up and wait. You have come prepared?"

"Yes," said Tharani, "I have brought vegetarian food cooked without ginger and garlic and onion. I've packed them in banana leaves."

The lady nodded approvingly. "You will be okay. Just make a circle with stones and wait."

"Is she scary?" asked Tharani.

The lady shook her head, "They are forest people. They are good."

"They?" asked Tharani, startled.

"Well, they're hill tribes. What did you expect?"

"I thought she was a Forest Spirit."

The lady laughed, "You could call her that. They're strange people, almost like animals, climbing trees and up the hill. She is one of them but she is the only one who will come out to meet people."

"Why only her?"

The lady shrugged. "We don't know what the rules are or whether they even have any homes or rules. You will like her. She is kind."

"Oh!" said Tharani, taking in all the information. "Do a lot of people come here?"

"No," said the lady, and her eyes hardened and the smiled vanished. "Not even desperation will bring anyone here to this lonely place. It takes a kind of temperament to do that."

"What kind?" asked Tharani coldly, sensing the hostility.

"The kind that is not afraid to die. The kind that is capable of anything."

Tharani stared coldly and steadily back at the lady. She understood that the woman meant that she was capable of murder. What would she know? She, who had never been uprooted from her country, never knew what it was to lose everything and start from scratch.

"Why are you here?" she asked the lady.

"I'm the station master. I've been posted here. I shall leave by the afternoon train and a railway guard will take over. He will also leave by the 6.30 train. It is the last one." She did not warn Tharani that if she missed that train, she would be alone here in the night and there was no electricity. "Anyone who had the guts to come to a place like this had surely braced themselves against all odds," she reckoned. Coming here meant they were okay with being alone in complete darkness with the possibility of being eaten up by animals or being raped or murdered. They had bought themselves a one-way ticket, especially someone like Tharani who had actually come without knowing anything for sure.

Tharani picked up her bag and made her way out of the station. The woman called out to her, "If you're carrying any weapons, you'll be killed. If you're unarmed, you will be protected."

Tharani paused. She then came back to the woman, took out a knife from within her blouse and handed it to her. She then took out another one tied to her skirt and gave that one too. She then put her hand inside the big bag that she had folded over the food. She took out a small pistol and gave that one too. The lady looked on with horror but had the wisdom to keep quiet.

Tharani then turned swiftly and left the station. The hills started abruptly from the station. Thankfully, the slope was gradual and she was able to climb to quite a distance without much difficulty. But soon, she entered the forest part of it and the trees grew close together and there was little sunlight. It grew progressively darker as she moved uphill, now very slowly and painstakingly, for it was quite steep. She stopped several times to catch her breath. She looked up and saw a kind of clearing a little further. She decided that was her destination. She took a deep breath and continued to climb till she reached it. It was quite a bit of open space, almost circular. She placed her bag on the ground, and sank thankfully to the ground and took deep breaths, till her breathing normalized. She looked around. She could see tiny rocks all over, so she picked up some and made a circle around herself, wide enough to allow her to sit comfortably. She then removed the big cloth bag, set it within the circle and placed the bag of food outside. She had brought a bottle of water. She took a swig and then sat down and waited. She did not feel the least bit foolish in all that she did. It was faith that had brought her this far, and faith made it all very real to her.

She was there a good two hours, just sitting there. It was all very peaceful although not very quiet. They were all natural sounds, of birds singing, squirrels squeaking, crows cawing. Thankfully, and strangely, no monkeys had appeared and taken pot shots at the food. In fact, she had not seen a single monkey. Squirrels ran around, birds chirped, branches swayed in the breeze, but these things apart, it was all very peaceful. Twice, she heard the rumble of a distant train. And then, suddenly, the birds flew up into the sky in alarm and she looked up. She heard a rustling noise. And then, she saw what appeared to be a white light moving swiftly from tree to tree towards her. Her heart raced and jumped to her mouth. She got up to her feet, and then stood transfixed. The light was now quite bright, a soft glow. It stopped at about 10 feet from her. As her eyes focused, she could see that it was a woman. The woman glowed! She emanated a soft radiant glow. Tharani had never seen a stranger sight. She saw a very beautiful woman of indefinite age. The figure was perfect and lithe and athletic. She was naked except for a skirt of some sort made out of leaves waist down. She had a chain of wild flowers around her neck. Her hair flew wildly around her face, surprisingly soft and shiny. Her skin was dark and flawless and glowing. Her features were perfect. But it was her eyes that drew Tharani's attention as they focused so strongly on her. "Sea green," she said under her breath. But as she stared, it became clear that the white of the eye was actually yellow and the pupils were deep blue "Yellow and blue!" Tharani exclaimed under her breath. The Spirit stood there, nonchalant and at ease, sizing her up. And then she smiled, showing perfect and even white teeth. Tharani folded her hands in homage, knelt down to the ground, and bent down so her head touched the ground. She then got up to her feet. She decided that this was indeed the Forest Spirit for although it was quite clear that she was a woman, she was definitely not an ordinary human being. The Spirit came forward to stand quite close to Tharani, but still out of the circle. Tharani could smell the faint, fading fragrance of the flowers around her neck, and some other, very pleasant bodily smell. She could feel the strength and vibrancy of the Spirit at close quarters. The Spirit then smiled at her again. She said something in a high-pitched voice, and then started dancing around the circle. She chanted as she danced. She then stopped once again in front of Tharani, reached out, and placed a hand on her head. And while Tharani had almost died of fright just moments earlier, she felt a peace descend on her the kind she had never felt in her life but had always longed for. It felt like all her longings, cravings, and searches ended in this all-engulfing white peace. Her heart beat slowed down and became steady and rhythmic. She felt protected and safe.

They stayed in a state of timelessness, thoughtlessness, connected, and only feeling. Then, slowly, slowly, the Spirit withdrew her hand, first easing the pressure, and then, removing her hand. And she smiled deeply into Tharani's eyes, and Tharani felt she was in the presence of one who loved her deeply, understood her, and did not judge her for who she was. She felt like a child in the presence of its mother. The Spirit then bent and took the food basket, and gestured to Tharani. "Wait here," Tharani interpreted. She nodded, "I will wait." And in one swift movement of light, the Spirit disappeared.

Tharani waited again, this time leaving the circle to find a place to pee. She then came back to within the circle. She was quite hungry. She had eaten in the train but it now seemed like a long time back. But there was nothing to eat. She had not kept any of the food for herself as she did not know if it was right to do so. So she drank some water and waited. Hours passed and it grew darker. Tharani was aware that it was evening, maybe early evening. She might miss the train, but there was nothing she could do about it. She dared not leave. But soon after, she again heard the rustle of leaves, and in swift movements of light, the Spirit appeared once again. This time, she came straight to Tharani. She had a basket woven out of palm leaves. She placed the basket within the circle and Tharani could see that there were leaves, fruits, twigs, and flowers in it. She looked askance at the Spirit and the Spirit gestured.

"Grind," interpreted Tharani, "Then take a little bit. Add to water. Give to drink. You don't drink. Okay?"

She nodded to the Spirit, "Okay."

And she once again folded her hands and knelt and bent so her head touched the ground. When she got up, the Spirit had left.

She picked up the palm basket, placed it within the big bag that she had brought, and left for the station.

The railway guard looked at her from above his horn-rimmed spectacles. He was in his white and white uniform, a rather nondescript man in his late fifties, possibly retiring soon. He then went back to his newspaper and to doing sudoku. He had seen crazy females before and wasn't surprised at all.

"When is the train coming in? asked Tharani.

"Half-past six," he said, not looking up.

"I'm hungry." said Tharani. He pushed a biscuit packet that was on the table towards her.

"Do you want some tea?" he asked.

"Yes."

"You can make some there." He pointed to a side of the room where there was an oil stove, a kettle, two cups and saucers, some tea, milk powder, and sugar. "Could you please make some for me too?"

Tharani nodded. She made two cups of tea, set one in front of him. She opened the biscuit packet, took three biscuits and setting them on her saucer, walked out to sit on the bench outside.

The train arrived almost on the dot at half-past six. The railway guard showed his flag, and it stopped. Tharani had earlier washed the cups and saucers, and the man had taken his bag out and locked the door to the room.

So now, all they had to do was board the train. He waited for Tharani to get in and he followed her. He watched her make her way with her bag to an empty seat. He followed, shaking his head and muttering to himself, "Crazy women! Only these many reasons why they do such things. Man there, man not there. Man good, man not good."

CHAPTER 4

*'tis your love, that's all I need; for the rest I am mute-
basking in your Moonlight, my own life silhouette*

The flats were a 'double deluxe'...or so the agent declared: two bedrooms, a nice, big hall, marble flooring, plenty of shelves, and a spacious, well-fitted kitchen. Perfect for a nuclear family. Theirs was on the second floor.

As they stood across the street, surveying the building, they noticed that on the ground floor, two women were seated at the doorsteps, plucking the leaves off of the stems of greens. Tharani knew one of them and her eyes brightened. Karishma, a lady she had often seen at the temple but had never spoken to. Indeed, she did not have the courage to do so. The haughty looking and extremely beautiful woman was the daughter of the Zamindar of Kayakote Village, a village well known for upholding its traditions and caste system even while allowing progressive times to prevail. Thus, even while the rich possessed the latest models in cars and phones and knew how to use the Internet, the village was still divided into sections according to caste, with the lower-most castes living outside a barbed wire fence that formed the border of the village. The village was famous for the quality of rice produce as well as for mangoes, which were a hybrid variety and extremely delicious and big. And this lady sitting there at her doorstep was the only daughter of the Zamindar. Upper caste, money, and beauty: God had indeed blessed her abundantly! She looked proud and arrogant, but when someone was blessed with so much, to Tharani, a little arrogance seemed justified. And now, she was going to live in the same building as this woman. What an opportunity to forge a friendship! This time, however, Tharani's calculations were not monetary. Respectability and acceptance, those so elusive qualities in her life, especially by those she considered bourgeois, was high on the list of her dreams. Money was just a means towards that end. In her mind, she liked to think she belonged to the upper circle.

Meanwhile, the two women had not noticed the family. They continued to clean the greens they had bought that morning. They each had placed the greens in a 'morom,' a kind of tray made by weaving wood slakes. The morom is closed on three sides and open and flat on the fourth side. It also slants slighted towards the open side. The morom dons several roles through the day in the hands of the efficient housewife. Farmers too use this to separate grain from chaff. They hold the grains to the wind and shake the morom from side to side, and the chaff flies away, leaving the grains. The housewife uses the morom to clean rice, vegetables, etc.

At the end of the day, the morom would possibly hold the ingredients for next day's cooking.

"I am going to mash the greens," said Karishma. She was married to a businessman and now lived in Madras.

"I'm not going to do that. I'm going to cut them thin and nice and cook them and add grated coconut," said Rashmi. Rashmi was a very pretty young Christian woman, newly married. Her parents lived in Bombay. She belonged to a middle-class family, and her husband was a techie.

"The coconut for this should never be grated in a mixer."

They both agreed.

"Yes, the brown part of the coconut gets grated too and that takes away from the presentation. I love the contrast of perfect white against perfect green."

"Not just that. The coconut gets kind of mashed up too much in a mixer. You need it to look flower-like or snowflake-like for the greens. Best grated with a manual grater."

They discussed the merits of the manual grater versus the electrical mixer.

"I'm making eggplant curry."

"Full ones?"

"Yes. I've slit the eggplants from the narrow end to the broad part both ways, like a cross. That keeps them whole and allows the spices in at the same time."

"Isn't it done from the broad part to the narrow?"

"No!" That's the wrong way to do it."

"My mom used to make it from broad to narrow."

Rashmi giggled. "What?" asked Karishma.

"What does it matter which way it's done? It all goes into the stomach."

They giggled like schoolgirls.

"You know that old lady upstairs?"

"The old accountant's wife?"

"Yes, that one. Well, she was asking me about condoms."

Rashmi looked wide-eyed, "Whatever for? And what did you say?"

"Asked me to show her. Said she'd never seen one, didn't know what it was. It wasn't there in her generation."

Rashmi giggled. "That's true. That's why they had so many kids. Four kids."

"That's rubbish! Contraceptive can't be everything. You've got to have self-control!'

"Do you have self-control?"

"Yes. We're very self-controlled. Except on days when he comes home with halwa and jasmine flowers."

"Aha!"

They giggled.

"Did you show her?"

"Yes. She wanted me to open the packet and show her."

They giggled some more.

"She wanted to know how it worked."

"For God's sake! She has four children!"

"Aha. And she has never used a condom."

"And you're the expert."

"Aha."

They giggled some more.

Then Rashmi exclaimed, looking across the street.

"Hey, look! What a beautiful family!"

And indeed they were! Sushanth and Tharani and the three girls stood across the road.

"She is so beautiful! Like some Hindu Goddess."

"Yes, I know. Looks can be so deceptive."

"What do you mean?"

"You know that banker who committed suicide? The one who lived in Mulla Street?"

"Yes. They said his family left him after he had an affair with some…oh!!"

"Right."

"Oh!" Rashmi looked with interest across the road. "But she really looks so lovely! And look at the kids! So beautiful, all of them!"

"Beauty with purpose."

"But it can't be, Karishma. The man was to blame too. And how do you know all this?"

"She comes to the temple every Tuesday. Barefeet. She does some strenuous poojas, like rolling on the ground. Likes to associate with people like me."

"You? Rich people."

"Yes, that too, but mainly people of upper caste. Likes to think she's one of us, upper caste and all. She always says, "We people…""

"You've spoken to her?"

"Nah! Some of my friends told me."

"What caste is she?"

"Who knows? She's a castaway from Burma."

They giggled.

"It's going to be interesting, hey?"

"Be careful."

"What do you mean? Why should I be careful?"

"A man is dead, a family broken. Sounds ruthless to me."

Karishma snorted, "She'd better not try any tricks with me. I'm likely to download a cartload of pure blood upper caste thugs on her from my village. And then she'd be running for her life."

"People like these, they don't stab you directly. They stab you, and you won't even know you're stabbed."

"That's a bit true, I guess. They say she has powers."

"Powers? Like through penances?"

"Maybe those, but more like spells and chants."

"Hmmm..."

"You don't believe me, do you? You're a city-born person. Come to our village. You'd know all about black magic."

"Hmmmm..."

"Anyways, I'm going to enjoy this."

"Like I said, be careful. The children look so adorable. Do you think they know?"

"They would, of course. Children always sense things. I had a friend whose husband was a sex maniac. He used to lock up the kids and then abuse his wife. The kids knew. One of the boys raped a girl and is locked up."

"Such things happen in this world. Why can't things be simpler?"

"There's only one reason, isn't it?"

"What's that?"

"Greed."

"And lust."

"Ah, yes! And cruelty too."

The next day was "shifting day," and Yamini, Sitara, and Sheila were excited. They helped enthusiastically to carry things to the second floor. Most of it went via the lift. Some of it had to be manually taken up. Sheila and Sitara ran up and down, getting in the way of the men, but quite sure in their minds that they were helping. "Hey! What's your name?" asked Karishma, as Sheila traipsed past.

"Sheila," she replied, looked back and smiled and ran up the stairs.

"Beautiful children."

"Yes," agreed Karishma.

Finally, it was all done. Sushanth was upstairs, unloading and putting things in their place. Tharani walked in at the ground floor landing. She smiled at Karishma, who smiled back, but with evident reserve. Rashmi's smile was open and welcoming. "Hi," she said. Tharani looked at her and smiled. "If you need anything, do let us know."

"Thank you! I will. I have to go up and see what the situation is like. Shifting is so difficult."

"Yes," Rashmi agreed politely.

Karishma smiled too. "Would you like some tea?"

Tharani brightened. The lady had spoken, she was offering tea!

"If you don't mind, yes. Tea would be good."

"Please go up and continue with your unpacking. I'll bring up some tea."

"Thank you!"

After Tharani had gone, Rashmi turned to Karishma in surprise, "You offered tea? I thought you didn't like her."

"Oh don't be such an innocent. Of course, I like her."

"No you don't. You're just curious."

Karishma shrugged, "All for good purpose."

Rashmi got up and shook the greens off her nightie. "You're a jobless curious cat."

Karishma smiled but said nothing.

With passing days, it became clear to Rashmi that Karishma and Tharani had more in common. She, the city-bred girl, could not talk about rituals or fasting or endlessly about recipes or gossip about neighbours. They talked for hours, they went out together to the market and temple. From her viewpoint, Rashmi could make out that their conversations were intimate, the way it could only be between very close friends. Rashmi, however, grew closer to the children, especially to Sitara, whose tomboyish nature appealed to her.

Finding herself slightly routed out and left out of conversations, Rashmi started going for walks and soon got to know quite a few of her other neighbours from the other apartments who were, like her, city-bred and more sophisticated. She started spending more time with them and soon they were a gang of women who did things together. Little did she know that Karishma was jealously watching the development.

It was Tuesday morning. The children had left for school. Sushanth had gone back to Bombay. He was now a partner too and owned the Chandni Supermarket along with Vineeth. He only came to Madras once in a couple of months or so and stayed for three or four days. It worked out well for them that Tharani stayed in Madras with the children. It demarcated quite well the source of the capital from the investment, so to speak.

Tharani had a bath and wore a beautiful blue cotton sari that she had bought recently. She picked up her basket of flowers and prepared to go to the temple. As usual, she did not wear her slippers. She closed the door and locked it. She was just about to get into the lift, but decided to take the stairs instead for exercise. She could hear women talking. Rashmi and Karishma were there on the ground floor, at their respective doorsteps, talking. Just as she moved to the first floor, she heard Karishma say, "I can't share what is mine with anyone. I'm a possessive woman. I don't want you being friends with anyone else. I can't take it."

"But you've moved on too," pointed Rashmi. "You and Tharani are such good friends now. You have more in common too."

"Seriously? You don't understand what's going on?"

"No…" Rashmi's uncertain voice.

"I'm playing a game with her. She thinks she's at par with me. She wants to be my equal. And I'm treating her that way."

"Why would you do that if you don't think that way," came Rashmi's shocked response, "It's not honest."

"Don't be silly. I'm just having some fun. When the time comes, she'll find out on her own. She won't be able to keep up, and then she'll know."

"It sounds quite cruel to me. She may be doing shady things but that's her business. If we didn't like her, no one is forcing us to be friends with her. Personally, I like her as a neighbour right now. I haven't seen anything going on yet."

"It will start. She just hasn't found a sucker yet."

"Be careful Karishma. These things are dangerous."

"Oh, don't worry about me. I'll be alright." The tone was careless and arrogant.

Tharani bent down and removed her anklets. She then quietly made her way back upstairs and into her house. She went in and sat on a chair, allowing...not diffusing...the fury to build up within her. Her nostrils flared, her eyes burned, her hair became frizzy; it was the demonic rage of a thwarted woman. She went into the bedroom and climbed up the bed and reached to the top shelf and retrieved a small book. She dusted it and sat down with it. It was a book of various chants and black magic. She turned it to a page and read through. And she sat there in deep contemplation.

Half an hour later, having calmed down completely, she picked up her basket of flowers and closed the door and made her way downstairs again. She could hear the women still talking but they had moved to other topics. She moved slowly downstairs. When she turned down the final flight of stairs, both women looked up and smiled. Tharani's eyes, however, were fixed on Karishma and she was staring at her in a strange manner. Then she smiled sweetly at her. "Good morning Tharani Ji," said Rashmi. Tharani turned to her. It was a strange fact but true that Tharani had never really even looked in Rashmi's direction before. To her, she was just another city-bred young girl, nothing very special. They had very little in common. But today, when she smiled at Rashmi, Tharani's smile was warm and motherly. There was gratitude in her heart for being respected and accepted. Her very soul craved respect and evaluation.

"I will be coming a little later to the temple Sheila Ma," said Karishma. She always called Tharani that. "It's a bit crowded today I heard. The head priest is coming."

Tharani nodded.

"Will you hold a place for me, please? I will try to be there in half an hour."

So broken was Tharani's spirit that when she again nodded her head, it was the servile nod of one stationed very low in life. "I will."

She moved past them, but Rashmi stopped her. "Tharani Ji, I'm leaving for Bombay tonight. Anil has left for America and he'll be gone for two months. And I think I'm pregnant."

"Oh!" said Tharani, genuinely pleased. She came back to Rashmi. "You will be blessed, I'm sure. You're a very good person. God Bless you."

"Why, thank you, Tharani Ji! I'll be back in a couple of months and I'm depending on you to take care of me."

"I will," Tharani promised. "You take care meanwhile."

Later that day, once she returned from the temple, Tharani locked her door and once again picked up the book. "Make a star with a chalk piece," it read. She did that right in the middle of the hall. "Place a lime at the centre." She placed the lime. "Now, get something that has been touched by the victim…"

She thought for a while, then made her way quietly downstairs and knocked on Karishma's door. "Yes, Sheila Ma, what is it?"

"Karishma, could you please give me back the small dish I gave you? I'm expecting some guests, so…"

"Oh, yes, of course! So sorry! I forgot." And Karishma went into the kitchen and came back with a small stainless-steel dish with some cooked vegetable in it. "I tried out a new recipe with pumpkin today. Please taste it and tell me how it is. It's okay to eat pumpkin today. It's just the first Tuesday. You can't eat pumpkin on the second and fourth Tuesdays."

"Thank you," said Tharani, taking the dish from her. "I'll let you know for sure."

She then made her way upstairs, while Karishma looked after her thoughtfully. She sensed that Tharani was not being very forthcoming. Tharani suddenly turned back as she reached the top of the stairs. "Karishma, what ingredients did you use?"

Thus reassured, Karishma told her the ingredients and the process, and the women stood there talking, to all appearances the best of friends.

Tharani went back upstairs and closed and locked the door. She then placed the dish with the cooked vegetable at the centre of the star. And then, she performed a most diabolic ritual that included chants and dancing.

The next day, Tharani went downstairs by the lift and was leaving to go shopping. She sniffed. The odour was faint. "Leaking gas," she surmised. There were only two houses in the ground floor and Rashmi's house was locked as she had left for Bombay the previous night. Karishma's door was open, and she sat there on the sofa, peeling peas. The odour came from her house. Tharani opened her mouth to warn her, then stopped suddenly. She remembered that Karishma had anosmia, the inability to perceive odour. She could not smell the gas. Tharani could not believe this was happening. Surely, it could not be this easy? Surely, her rituals were not working?

"Hello, Karishma. Feeling lonely?"

"Yes, Sheila Ma. Rashmi has left for Bombay. My husband has gone to Bangalore. His sister lives there. She has some problems, and he's gone to be with her."

"And Madan has gone to school?"

"Yes." Madan was Karishma's ten-year-old son.

"All my kids are in school too. Some peace," smiled Tharani.

"Yes, that's true!" Karishma laughed. "We miss them when they're not there, and when they're here, they trouble us so much."

"Yes," smiled Tharani. And all the while, the gas odour was increasing.

"Well, I'd better be going. I'm going shopping with some friends from Burma."

"Okay, Sheila Ma. Have a great time."

When she reached the end of the landing, Tharani stopped, human kindness and concern prevailing. She turned back to look at the woman sitting innocently on the sofa, all alone, peeling peas. A small aluminium plate was placed near the door. She looked curiously at the plate.

"What is that plate for?" she asked.

"Oh, a field worker is coming from my village today. My parents are sending me some rice and other things through him, harvests from our own fields. He is of a lower caste and cannot come into the house or eat from our vessels. This is for him. I am cooking separately for him."

Tharani looked at the plate and then at Karishma. "Don't you think that's inhuman? We treat animals better."

"Oh, they don't mind. They know and accept it. They are pretty much like animals."

Tharani could not help but stare at the arrogant woman. She then shook herself as if out of a reverie. "Well, I'll be going."

"Yes, see you in the evening, Sheila Ma."

Tharani nodded her head, turned and left, muttering to herself, "I don't think."

After shopping, she made her way to the temple, unwilling to go home. And that is where she found groups of women standing outside and talking in shocked tones, "She died on the spot. Not much left of her. The blast was terrible. Quite a leak, I heard…."

CHAPTER 5

to find a way through darkness, an endless fight
no respite, no respite, on a moonless night

"Please sit properly Sitara!"

Sitara was seated on a chair with both feet propped on a side table that was at a higher level than her chair. She had on a short skirt that had moved back to reveal her panties. She was reading a book, and she ignored her mother's order and continued to read.

"Sitara! I said…"

"I heard you." But she still did not move.

"Sitara, move right now!"

Sitara lifted her legs down and shut her book. She turned to her mother. "If not what? You'll beat me up, is that it?"

"Don't talk to me like that!"

Yamini and Sheila, who were seated at the dining table, watched, wide-eyed.

"Okay, I'm sorry. It's not correct to show one's panties, right?"

Tharani coloured, "Yes. You have to learn to sit gracefully. You're growing up."

"Thank you for letting me know that! Otherwise how would I have known?"

"Why the sarcasm Sitara? What have I done?"

Sitara shook her head restlessly, "I don't know! …I don't know. I just think it's funny the way we've shifted like this, so soon after Karishma Aunty died."

"Our shifting has nothing to do with her death."

"She was your friend. You were with her so much of the time."

"Yes, and I'm sorry about what happened to her."

"But you must have known!"

"I wasn't there, Sitara. I went out shopping."

"But you must have gone to the landing to leave. Didn't you smell the gas then?"

Tharani started despite herself, her eyes wide.

"There was no smell when I left."

"You're sure? Because Karishma Aunty had anosmia. She wouldn't have smelt anything. But you would have."

"Are you trying to implicate that I knew but kept quiet? Is that what you're saying?"

"I don't know Mom! Seems strange that she died the way she did."

"That's enough. I'll have none of your cheek! Stop talking rubbish and get back to your studies."

Sitara opened her mouth to argue but caught Yamini's eyes and retreated. Sheila looked up at Yamini, a scared look on her face. She hated confrontations; they terrified her. Yamini smiled and said soothingly, "It's okay. She's just tired and cranky." Sheila nodded. "Go in and finish your homework. I'll come in later and take a look." Sheila left the table with alacrity. She was too small to understand what was going on but she sensed that something wasn't quite right. But apparently Yamini thought it was all going to be okay. Yamini was always right.

Tharani was more worried and scared that she was willing to admit. They had shifted to a new house a month after Karishma's death. Rashmi was not back yet, but Tharani received a call from her. She had sobbed over the phone. And then, she had begun saying something, but her voice had trailed off, "I warned her…."

Tharani had not dared to ask what she had warned Karishma about. "I'm sorry, there's someone at the door, Rashmi. I'll call you later." She had hung up.

Careful not to raise any suspicions, she waited a couple of months, and then shifted her family to an apartment right at the end of the colony. Sushanth had come down to help with the move and had gone back to Bombay. They were now quite comfortably settled in the new place, an apartment, once again, on the second floor.

However, there was a subtle change in the behaviour of both the older girls, Yamini and Sitara. Yamini did not protest outright, but she tried to avoid her mother if she could. She buried herself in her books, spoke more to Sitara and Sheila, and kept a distance from Tharani. Sitara, on the other hand, was openly insolent.

"They sense something," thought Tharani, biting off the thread. She was stitching a blouse. "They're not sure what it is, but they sense it." She pondered whether this was a good thing or a bad thing. "They'd come to know sooner or later. I could not have kept anything from them. Not about Karishma though. That was a bolt from the blue what Sitara said. The girl is too sharp for her age. She's only twelve, for God's sake! Too observant for her own good. But the other thing, Sharma ji's suicide...they'd have to know about that. I can't hide that from them forever."

"It's best," she concluded. "This is the reality of their existence too. They'd have to learn sooner or later that we live by different rules. In fact, rules act like obstacles sometimes..." She turned the blouse inside out. It didn't occur to her that there were hundreds of immigrants in the country who lived by the rules and still managed to settle down quite nicely.

That night, after dinner, Sitara went out of the house, banging the door shut as she left.

"Where is she going?" asked Tharani, "Call her back in. She can't bang the door like that."

Yamini came over to her. "She's gone to the terrace, ma. Please relax. I'll talk to her."

They looked at each other. This was their first normal interaction since they'd moved to the new house. Tharani was closest to her eldest daughter and tended to confide in her, knowing she would not be judged. She had missed that more than she was willing to admit. She wanted to plead with Yamini not to judge her, but it turned out there was no need for her to do that. The girl's eyes held nothing but gentle compassion. Tharani nodded gratefully. "Talk some sense into her."

"I'll try."

Yamini went to the terrace and looked around. She found Sitara standing near the wall on one side and staring at the street lights that overlapped the stars and owned the sky. For a moment, Yamini felt her heart leap to her mouth in terror. Was Sitara trying to commit suicide? But she wasn't moving...she was just standing there and staring.

"Hi," said Yamini, tentatively, as she moved to stand beside her, "What..." she stopped. Sitara was still crying.

"Hey!" said Yamini, "Why're you crying? Is something bothering you?"

Yamini was a simple and direct person. She did not mince words nor did she overuse them.

Sitara shook her head. After a while, she turned to Yamini, "They're being so rude to me!"

"Who?"

"The kids in my class. You know the son of that banker who hanged himself? His name is Ashok. Ashok Sharma. He's my junior—Class 7. He told everyone that mom is responsible for his father's death. He says she seduced him."

"You know what seduction means?"

"Oh, come on, Yami! I'm not a kid!"

Yamini smiled, "I thought you were....but continue."

"No one's talking to me. Yesterday, I washed my hands and came in for lunch. They had emptied out my food and thrown the box in a corner. My bag was hanging over the door."

"That bad?"

"Worse!"

I'm so sorry, Sit. I didn't know. I'll look in on Monday. I'm not having a great time either. No one will talk to me. They're not willing to share notes either. I have to figure out everything on my own."

"I don't want this, Yami! I can't take it anymore!"

Yamini was silent. She looked into the horizon. Then she said simply, "I can."

Sitara turned to her in horror, "What!? How!? You can't go on in a place like that! You can't survive!"

"I can because I know that if she did what they say she did, it's because of me."

She turned to Sitara. "Suddenly it's become affordable for them to send me to school and Daddy has become a partner with Vineeth Uncle now. All that's happened after…you know. If she did it for me, I can take it. I will."

"But what she did was wrong! You can't live off…sponge off someone!"

"Takes two for a seduction to happen, Sit. You can't seduce a man who doesn't want to be seduced."

Sitara turned back to the street lights in the horizon. Then she threw back her head arrogantly, shaking her hair like a wild horse's mane, and stated, "I can!"

Yamini looked at her younger sister, then threw back her head and laughed, "You wretch!"

Sitara looked at her sister laughing and she laughed too. Their childish laughter rang through the cold, silent night. Sitara put her head on Yamini's shoulder and Yamini put her arms around Sitara, "You know, these are not the people who are going to certify me. It's board exams, and as for my character, they don't have a thing against me. I'll work my way out. I'll study hard and pass my exams and go to college and become an engineer. And then I'll take care of you and Sheila and Mom and Dad."

A hand came up to her face and poked her eyes, "Ouch!"

Sitara looked up from her comfortable perch, "You forgot an important fact. I'd be working too."

"So you're okay with what mom did…does?"

"We're immigrants, Sit. We work by different rules. Have you seen her buy anything for herself? She fasts, she goes barefoot to the temple… She's thinking of us all the time: clothes for us, food for us, nice house for us, and good education. If we let her down, everything she's done this far becomes meaningless."

"That' true! I didn't think of that. What about Karishma aunty, Yami? I really feel she had something to do with it."

"She didn't, Sit. Maybe she didn't tell her the gas was leaking…That we'll never know."

"And that doesn't strike you as wrong? It sounds like murder to me."

"She wasn't a very nice lady. She set Mom up."

"Set her up? How?"

"Well, she pretended to be Mom's friend, but all the while, she was trying to put Mom down as being a lower caste person. She was making fun of her behind her back."

"How do you know?"

"I heard Mom crying the night before Aunty died. I asked her and she told me. I'm the eldest child, so she finds it easier to talk to. Sometimes, not always."

"Oh! Karishma Aunty did that?"

"Yes."

"Bitch!"

"But that doesn't make it alright if mom knew the gas was leaking and didn't tell her," Yamini said.

Sitara's voice sounded doubtful now, "I don't know…"

"Sitara!"

Sitara grinned, "Relax. I know it's not alright. I wouldn't do a thing like that. I'd wish her in hell though. I understand Mom's anger, especially after being mistreated in school."

Yamini sighed, "I dream of growing up, Sit. I dream of getting past all this and being my own person, with a job and a house and…"

"Taking care of all of us. What about marriage?"

Yamini shook her head. "I won't get married. It wouldn't work after what's happened in our lives." She turned to Sitara, voicing her deepest fear, "This is just the beginning of things, Sit. We haven't been involved…yet." She hesitated, and then she said, her voice trembling, her eyes bright with unshed tears, "We might be."

"What do you mean involved?" asked Sitara.

And then her eyes widened, "You mean…?"

Yamini shrugged, "We're not children anymore."

Sitara opened her mouth to protest, and then stopped. The gravity of what Yamini was trying to tell her dawned on her. And in that one moment, the girls grew up and became women.

The next day, after the children had left for school, Tharani got ready and went out shopping with Shanthi. She and Shanthi had become quite close, supporting each other in the absence of their husbands. They went out together quite often and kept in touch. They never discussed their personal nefarious activities, but it remained an understanding between them. Shanthi was currently involved with a rich diamond merchant who lived uptown. The man had a large family and a big well-known shop in the heart of the city, but he liked to have a little fun on the side. It cost him a few diamonds' worth, but on the whole, it was no very big pinch on his pocket. His family, especially his wife, was aware of his adventures, but chose not to react as is the way with a lot of women who are middle-aged or older and know no other life and are not educated enough to be confident that they can be financially independent at any point. The fact that in India, the girl's family washes it's hands clean when she is married off and makes it very clear to her that she now 'belonged' to her husband's family, did not help any. The woman, mostly, had no fall back plan and chose to remain silent and continue with the only life she knew. She had made her peace with it, and, in some ways, she felt it helped the monotony of their marriage. He certainly was more lenient now and allowed her more freedom; he was less possessive, and yet, guilty enough to take good care of her. Not much to complain about really.

The arrangement suited Shanthi as well as there was a steady flow of income. Besides, the supermarket in Bombay was doing well, and soon there would be no need for her or Tharani to try this hard.

As they walked along the road towards the bus stand, they passed a shop, which was actually more of a store place of grains and pulses. A little further from the shop, a young man in his mid-twenties stood talking to three beautiful young teenage girls. The laughter, body language, and expression, all indicated that he was trying to flirt.

Shanthi nodded towards the group. "See that boy over there," she said to Tharani, "He's the only son of a zamindar. All the products you see there in the shop are from their lands. He has a sister. She's to be married to another landlord. Useless, good-for-nothing playboy, always going after girls. His father is trying to teach him responsibility. That's why he's sent him down here to take care of this shop. They have several shops. He's supposed to learn discipline. A supervisor comes in twice or thrice a week to check in on him.

Tharani listened intensely, "He doesn't look like he's learning anything."

"Yeah, he's having fun. When things come that easy to you…"

Shanthi turned to Tharani and an understanding passed between them. It was like, "Here's your sitting duck."

Meanwhile, the boy in question stood smiling at the three teenagers. His name was Ramesh.

"Yes, all the products are from my farm. We've got a lot of land."

"Obviously," said a quiet girl, who looked quite intelligent, "You're a landlord."

"We have animals too. Cows, pigs, horses… We have small animals too."

"What do you mean?"

"Well, we have a goldfish farm, and a duck farm."

"That's fantastic! Where's this wonderland?"

"In my village. I could take you all there one day if you'd like to come?"

The other two girls squealed with delight. "Of course we would!"

"I can't come," said the quiet girl, "My parents won't allow it."

"She's not allowed to go anywhere," said another girl.

"I'm sorry to hear that," said Ramesh. He turned to the other two, "What about you?"

"Oh, we'll come for sure. Let us know a date."

"Sure," said Ramesh, satisfied at the way things were going, "Meanwhile, how about I take you girls out to dinner?"

"Dinner? Well, that would be nice. But I'll have to check it out with my boyfriend."

"Oh…you have a boyfriend?"

"Yes" said the girl, laughing, "Does that put me out of the picture?"

"Well…"

"Well, what?" said the quiet girl, angrily, "You were hoping you'd have three girls in tow to choose from? If that's what you do, you can just move on! Come on girls, let's go!"

The other two girls got on their bikes rather reluctantly. They didn't mind if towing them and looking good was his thing. He sounded fun. What a spoilsport she was!

"I say! Don't go! Wait! I'm not that bad!"

But his pleas fell on deaf ears.

The supervisor, a huge hefty man who looked like a wrestler, came over.

"If you've had your fun, can we get back to numbers?" he said, sarcastically. He had been with the family a very long time and knew Ramesh since he was a baby. He had been given permission to treat the boy roughly if necessary.

"Okay, I'm coming." Ramesh walked dejectedly back to the shop.

"That didn't work out, eh?"

"No, it didn't. One was a prude, the other one had a boyfriend."

"What about the third one?"

"The prude spoilt it."

"Ah, well, you tried. Now come on, come here boy. See this is the cost price...."

Ramesh gave in ungraciously and got down to brass tacks. But once the supervisor had left, he just sat there and daydreamed about girls. He was a strange boy: tall, lanky, and handsome is a watery kind of way. He was rather giddy for his age, but intuitive and sensitive too. Although he was unaware of it, his charm lay in his inherent humility; he was a non-judgemental person who was willing to think the best of everyone, and was quite gentle. That combined with his wealth, status, and upbringing made him inherently charismatic. Perhaps later on, with a real purpose in life, he would be stronger and firmer, but it seemed that he was taking his own good time growing up and getting there.

"I want to buy some rice," said a husky voice.

Ramesh looked up. A lady stood there.

"Yes, please," said Ramesh, getting up. He came over to the front of the shop. "What kind of rice do you want?"

"I want raw rice. Can you show me some varieties?"

"Sure" said Ramesh, a little more enthusiastically. The lady was not young but she was beautiful. She had lovely features, was pleasantly wholesome. "Such eyes!" he thought, "Gold with dark flecks in them."

"I can show you quite a few varieties. See this one is a jasmine variety. It's been twice polished."

"Too much polishing is not good?"

"I agree with you. You could try this one; it is single polished. Or this one here, which is hand pounded and unpolished."

Tharani bent over a bag of rice and the pullo of her sari fell over. She seemed unaware of the fact as she continued to talk about rice and take some in her hand.

Ramesh stared transfixed at her breasts hanging low over the rice and his heart raced. The boy was a flirt but he had never been with a woman, not even this close.

Tharani got up and lifted her pullo casually and draped it once more over her shoulder.

She looked at him, "What about the one there."

"Ah...yes! Yes, please take a look."

And once more, Tharani bent over, and once more, her pullo fell down. But this time when she straightened up, she looked at Ramesh directly and an entirely sexual awareness passed between them. They stood there staring at each other, and a pact was made in that moment.

It was Ramesh who broke the contact. He moved to the other side of his desk, suddenly wishing to shield himself. "How much would you like to buy?"

"You sell wholesale, right?"

They were still aware of each other.

"Yes. But I could give you as less as one kilo."

"I'll take a five-kilogram bag."

"Okay. Will you carry it or shall I have it sent over?"

"I'll take it."

Ramesh left his perch and moved to the bags and measured out the rice. Tharani walked out of the shop and waited. He tied the bag and brought it over to her.

"Thank you," she said, looking up at him, and the awareness was back.

Once she left, he went back to his desk and sat down. What had just happened? The lady had made a pass at him! She'd thrown him a line! What in the world! And who was she?"

Ramesh was no fool. He didn't believe that a woman that age would flirt with him for no reason. He could quite as well be her son. She must want something. What? Money? If only he knew who she was.

He got his answer sooner than he expected. Just as Tharani was leaving the shop and down the street, the supervisor came back. He saw her carrying the bag of rice.

"That lady came to the shop?" he asked Ramesh, sharply.

"Yes. She wanted a bag of single polished rice."

"Well!"

"Why what's the matter? That's just a customer."

"Customer rubbish! She's a fleecer."

"Fleecer?"

"A parasite if ever there was one. She lures men, and then, before they know it, she's fleeced them off their money. Didn't you hear of the banker who committed suicide?"

"Yes, I did. Oh!"

"Please be careful, Ramesh. She's no simple miss. She means business."

"Sure. I'll be careful," said Ramesh, but in his heart, he was very excited. So she'd thrown him a line. She wanted to fleece him in return for...Wow!

What was a little bit of money in return for...?? He'd be learning so much! She was an experienced woman. Maybe it was all worth it.

Ramesh spent the rest of the afternoon conjuring up the picture of Tharani bent over the rice.

A week later, a schoolgirl of about 12 got down from her bicycle and came into the shop. She handed a bag and a tiffin box to Ramesh. "Mom told me to give you this," she said, tonelessly.

Ramesh looked at her and smiled, taking the bag and box from her, "Please thank her for me."

The girl looked at him with disdain and asked rather sarcastically, "You get kheer from your customers regularly?"

"No, I don't. Why?"

"You're acting like you know who my mom is."

"I do. Because you look just like her. Same beautiful eyes…"

"Right!" snorted Sitara, completely disgusted, "I should have known!"

"Does your mom give kheer to all the shopkeepers?"

"No," said Sitara, colouring and looking embarrassed. "It's her birthday today. And I guess she likes you."

"Nice! Please wish her on my behalf."

"Do it yourself," Sitara threw back her head and walked away. Then she stopped and turned and gave him a thoughtful look, "Just making a point: I'm not like my mom. Okay?"

Ramesh gazed back at her, understanding her dilemma and wanting to sooth, "Sure. I got that."

"So long as you did," she said and got on her bike and sailed away.

"Like mom, like child," said Ramesh to himself. "Like mom, like…" He opened the box. "Mmmm!! Delicious kheer! So what's next?"

He ate the kheer and cleaned up the box. "Next, of course, is that I take the box back to her and thank her. In person."

He rang the bell tentatively, and then moved in line with the peephole. Someone was looking at him. Then the door opened. Tharani stood there in a dark nightgown. She had been cooking and was slightly sweaty, "Come in" she said, "What a surprise!"

He went in and she closed the door. For a moment, he felt completely trapped and contemplated escaping; then he braced himself. He was a grown man for God's sake! Not a green, innocent child. Surely he could take care of himself?

"I brought you the box," he said, handing it over to her, "The kheer was delicious. Thank you!"

Tharani smiled. "You're welcome."

"I heard it's your birthday. I've brought you a little present."

He gave her the box. "Oh! You didn't have to!" she exclaimed. But she took it from him and went to the side table. She picked up a knife and slit open the package. It was a clay statue of a beautiful bathing woman. Her white transparent sari clung to her skin, marking brown here and there. Her hair was tied in a knot over the top of her head, with dark unruly ringlets that escaped and crowned her face. Water dripped from them over her shoulder, and she had one foot in a small puddle. It was a very beautiful work of art indeed.

Tharani looked at it in delight. "Wow! So beautiful!" she said. She loved beautiful things, being something of a connoisseur. "It's also very…sensuous," she said, thoughtfully, looking at him. He blushed and looked out the window. "Thank you so much! Please sit down."

Ramesh sat down. "Can I get you some tea?" asked Tharani.

"Ah, yes. Yes, I would like some tea," said Ramesh, looking hungrily at her. She did not miss the look.

"I'll be back." She went in and made tea. She brought it over and bent over him. He realized as she walked that she had removed her bra and that the front buttons of her nightgown were now open. Now, as she bent over him and handed him the cup of tea, he could see all the way down to her breasts. The musky natural body odour swamped him and he could barely hold on to his senses.

"The tea is just right," said the husky voice, as she looked directly into his eyes.

"Th..th…thank you,"

"Let go,"

"Uh?"

"Let go of control. It's going to be okay."

"It's…I…uh!"

"Come," and taking him by the hand, she led him to the bedroom. He followed her unresisting and docile, pretty much like the foolish lamb being led to be slaughtered.

raging storm, core on fire
reaching out
for the moon, the tide's desire

It started as a slight twinge in the lower abdomen, and Yamini ignored it at first. But by the second period post lunch, the pain had increased, and by the end of the period, it was quite unbearable.

"Yamini, what's the matter?"

"Ma'am, my stomach hurts."

"Oh! Come here."

Yamini left her place and went over to the teacher. "How bad is it?"

Yamini's lips trembled, "I can't bear it."

If it had been some other child, the teacher would have had doubts that they were making excuses to get to go home early, but this girl was one of her best students. "Apart from being so shy and introvertish," she thought. Aloud she said, "Go home, Yamini. You might need to see a doctor."

"Thank you, Ma'am."

Yamini picked up her bag and left the classroom.

She reached the apartment, took the lift, and knocked on the door.

She heard Tharani say, "Coming!" But the person who opened the door was a young man. He looked as blankly at her as she did at him.

"Yes?" he asked.

"I... I live here."

"Oh!" and he moved aside to let her in. Yamini walked in. Tharani came out of the kitchen carrying a cup of tea. She was surprised to see Yamini.

"Yamini! You're home early!"

Yamini nodded her head, and without saying another word, walked into her bedroom and locked the door.

Tharani came over and gave the cup of tea to Ramesh. "I think you'd better leave."

He nodded and took the teacup from her. But then, he sat down on the couch to drink his tea. Tharani went over to the bedroom door and knocked. "Yamini! Let me in! Yamini!"

The door opened and Yamini allowed her mother to come in before shutting it again.

"Who is that?" she asked.

"That's the boy from the rice shop. Ramesh."

"Oh... okay." Yamini was a sensitive young girl and she surmised quite correctly what he was doing in their house. She did not ask any awkward questions. Besides, her stomach still hurt very badly.

"My stomach hurts. I can't bear it." A tiny teardrop trickled down her cheek.

"Oh dear!" said Tharani, "It must be something you ate. Lie down, let me see."

She examined Yamini, then said, "It's in the lower abdomen. You have a stomach upset. Just lie down and shut your eyes. I'll make you a brew. It'll be alright in a jiffy."

Yamini nodded and closed her eyes. Tharani left the room.

"You're still here?"

"Yes," said Ramesh, looking blissful and settled on the couch. "How is she?"

"Stomach ache. I'm going to make her a brew."

"Oh! What will you use?"

He got up and followed her to the kitchen. Tharani looked uncertainly at him. She was not sure she wanted him there. Wasn't he supposed to leave? But she did not say anything.

"First you keep a bowl of water to boil. And then…"

She moved around as she spoke, filling a bowl with water.

"I'll cut the herbs. Is there anything you want that is not there?"

"Let me see. Yes, I need honey."

"I'll go get that."

"You will?"

"Yes. I have my bike."

Tharani looked at him curiously. Despite being in his twenties, there was a certain engaging innocence about him. She was dealing with a young person, nearer her children's age.

"Okay."

He nodded enthusiastically and left. He was back soon with a bottle of honey. Tharani filled a small bowl with the brew and then went and knocked on the bedroom door. She was startled to find Ramesh standing right behind her.

Forgetting the need to be polite and talking to him more the way she spoke to Sitara, she said, "That's enough. You go watch TV or leave. You can't come in."

He actually listened to her and obeyed.

Yamini drank the brew, and after a while, she did feel better.

When Yamini came out of her room later that evening, she was startled to find the young man still sitting there on the couch and watching TV. He was laughing loudly at something on a show.

She walked into her mother's bedroom. "Ma, why is he still here?"

Tharani looked up from her sewing machine, "I don't know."

Yamini sighed. "I suppose you can't ask him to leave."

Tharani did not answer her.

"I have to go to the hall to get my books."

Tharani looked at her daughter, her face crimson.

"I'll get them for you."

But Yamini shook her head, "I'll go. It's okay."

She went into the hall and to the table near the couch. Ramesh looked up at her. When he had opened the door to let her in, he had taken in only her overall appearance, and he hadn't been very impressed. He had decided that she was a rather plain-looking schoolgirl, quite dark, with long hair done in two plaits. She had now changed into loose-fitting pyjamas and a black T-shirt, neither of which did much for her appearance, but he couldn't help be distracted by the swinging grace with which she crossed the room.

She picked up her bag and turned to leave, "You're Yamini, right?"

She turned to look at him, "Yes."

"Which class?"

"I'm taking my board exams this year."

He nodded. She was close enough for him to see her face, and he was startled by the perfection of each feature as they registered on him. Perfect brows, beautiful brown eyes that gazed seriously at him, perfect nose, perfect lips, and a perfect oval face. "My God! This girl is so beautiful!" he thought.

Yamini had left by then. Ramesh went back to watching TV.

An hour later, the door went "Bang! Bang!" The bell rang incessantly, and a voice called out loudly, "Maaaaaaaaaaa!!"

Ramesh opened the door to find the twelve-year-old girl who had come to his shop and a younger one, about ten years old.

Sitara stared up at him, "You!!"

He grinned happily at her and stepped aside. She came in followed by Sheila. "Where's Ma?"

"In the bedroom."

"And why are you here?"

"I'm watching TV."

Tharani came out of the bedroom and Sitara turned to her angrily, "What is he doing here?"

"He's watching TV," said Tharani, trying to soothe her.

Sitara grabbed the remote out of Ramesh's hand and threw it on the couch. "Go and watch somewhere else."

"Sitara!" said her mother. "Go inside!"

"Oh! So I am the one who has to leave. And your boyfriend will stay here?"

"He is not…"

"Bah!" said the girl, and taking Sheila by her hand, she went into the bedroom and banged the door shut.

Tharani looked with distress at the closed door, then she turned to Ramesh, "I think you had better leave."

"Okay," he said, reluctantly. "I just want to finish watching this episode."

Tharani sighed, "Okay, you can. But leave right after."

He did not reply. He sat back on the couch, took the remote, and switched on the TV.

Tharani went to the bedroom and banged on the door…

And that is how things went on from there. Ramesh walked in and out of the house just like the other family members. He ran errands for them, settled down on the couch and watched TV, said he was hungry, and helped around the house and kitchen. He cut vegetables and cleaned up. The girls eventually grew resigned to it all. They all dropped any polite facade and treated him pretty much as a family member. "Get out my room!" and throwing a pillow at his retreating form became a normal interaction. He was particularly gentle and patient with Sheila, taking her for rides on his bike and buying her ice-creams and listening to her prattle.

"Divide it first, and then multiply."

Yamini looked up, startled, from the math problem she had been breaking her head over. "You're good at maths?"

Ramesh walked over to the other side of the table in the balcony where the girls were seated and studying. He sat down casually on the railing.

"Yes," he said simply.

"What have you studied?" asked Yamini

"I'm an engineer," again, quite simply.

"What!" said Sitara, "You're an engineer??!!"

He looked at her with a smile lurking in his eyes, "Why is that so impossible to believe?"

"Because you... you don't look like you're doing anything." Sitara was never diplomatic.

"I have a rice shop," he pointed out to her.

"Yes, but what has that to do with engineering? You're just selling rice!"

"Rice needs a lot of thinking, trust me."

Sitara snorted.

Yamini was looking at him with interest, "Why aren't you working in, like in a corporate office or owning your own company? Why aren't you using your degree?"

"I don't want to. I'm the only son of a landlord. My father takes care of everything now, but he's past sixty, and in a little while, I'll have to take over the responsibilities of running the estate. And right now, I have all the money I want anyways. Why would I work?"

The girls were silent. It sounded logical the way he said it. What it was to be that rich! Then Sitara asked, "So why did you get an engineering degree?"

"I need education. Knowledge is everything to us. Even apart from education, we read a lot, keep abreast of things... new technologies, policies... We keep ourselves updated."

"By "we" you mean your family?"

"Yes."

"Hasn't helped you much, has it?" said Sitara, sarcastically.

"Sitara!" said Yamini, shocked at her sister's outspoken rudeness.

But Ramesh only laughed, "I have a younger sister. Her name is Meenakshi. She's in college now, doing biochemistry."

"Oh!" said Yamini, immediately interested, "I intend to do that too!!"

He looked at her affectionately, "I'll help you in every way I can to get you there." She met his eyes and she knew he was sincere.

"Will your sister work... you know, as a biochemist?"

"That's her choice," said Ramesh. "She's already betrothed to the son of another landlord. It's all up to her and her in-laws."

"Will you help me with my homework?" asked Sheila.

"Of course, I will!" said Ramesh, and he went around to sit next to her.

From that day on, Ramesh helped the girls with their school work, especially with science and maths. Perhaps because he was closer to her age-wise than with the others, he grew closer to Yamini. He treated her as his equal, discussing her future with her, advising her, telling her about his dreams.

"This pin goes right there!" he stood close to her, bending over the table to place the pin. They were doing an experiment in reflection, with two mirrors placed over a chart.

"See if this is okay?"

Yamini bent over the table to his level to take a look. And suddenly, she was aware of the proximity. The pleasant aftershave fragrance wafted over. He wasn't muscular, but rather with wiry strength, and somehow she liked that. She liked the way she wore his shirt, the way he was always clean and well dressed...

Ramesh had move to the side to place the pin, and as he bent over, he caught a reflection of her in the mirror. There was desire written all over her face...

Their eyes met in the mirrors and got reflected multiple times... ..

Time stood still for a moment, and then, Yamini blushed, looked flustered, and ran out of the room. Ramesh looked thoughtfully at the pins in his hand.

It was the day after. The children had all gone to school and Ramesh was alone with Tharani that afternoon. Indeed, their affair had gone uninterrupted despite everything: the girls' friendliness, the disparity in age, and the fact that there was a husband somewhere in the midst of all this. Tharani had written to Sushanth about Ramesh, and he kept discreetly away. He came in two months later, on a weekend, and at that point, Ramesh kept away. It was all nicely arranged and the two men never met. Coincidentally, the supervisor who was supposed to be vigilant about Ramesh and report to his father about his whereabouts had been called off. Ramesh's father felt his son was doing quite a good job. He was selling well and the books showed good profits. It was a good beginning. And so, he had complied with Ramesh's insistent request that he be trusted.

"I want to show you something."

"What is it?" asked Tharani as she lay next to him in bed.

He leaned over and pulled his pants towards him. He reached into the pocket and pulled out a box and opened it. And embedded in satin, was the most beautiful necklace that Tharani had ever seen. It sparkled with white and red and green stones.

"Diamonds and rubies and emeralds," said Ramesh, looking up at Tharani's wonderstruck face.

"You mean real ones?"

"Yes. This belongs to my mother. It's a family heirloom." He looked at the chain. "Beautiful, isn't it?"

"It's gorgeous!" said Tharani, looking at him, "May I?"

"Yes, of course!"

She took the chain carefully out of the box and held it reverently in her hands. "So intricate!"

Ramesh looked at her. "Try it on."

"Me??"

"Yes. Why not?"

He reached for the chain and put it round her neck and fastened it at the back. She got up to look at herself in the mirror. Even in her current dishevelled state, she was beautiful, and the necklace shone around her neck. She could imagine how she would look with a beautiful silk sari on, hair coiffured, face with the lightest touch of makeup and her eyes highlighted....and the necklace on... and walking into a room full of people...

"Looks very nice on you," said Ramesh.

"Thank you!"

He came to stand behind her and looked at her in the mirror, "It would look lovely on Yamini too."

Her hand, which had lingered over the stones, stilled. There was an infinite pause as their eyes met in the mirror. And then, she was reaching behind to undo the clasp. She turned and gave the necklace back to him, looking directly and coldly into his eyes, "No."

He did not say anything, but just took the necklace from her and put it back in its box.

Tharani looked angrily at him, "How dare you?"

"Why, is that inappropriate?" It was a sarcastic comment for sure, but the way he said it, it sounded like a sincere query. "She likes me you know."

Tharani's eyes widened, "Why would you say that?"

He shrugged, and she knew that he could tell when a girl was interested in him.

"I think you'd better leave now."

He nodded and pulled on his clothes and walked to the door.

"Can you... can you just leave that here?" Tharani asked him, pointing to the box.

He hesitated a moment, then nodded and placed the box on the sewing machine table. "Please be careful. It's a family heirloom."

She nodded, "I will."

That evening, Tharani carried over a tea tray to the balcony where Yamini sat alone doing her homework. Sitara and Sheila had gone out to play. Tharani mixed the tea and set it next to Yamini's books.

"Drink your tea and have some toast. You need to relax some."

"I need to get these done today." Yamini looked up from her work. She suddenly caught sight of the glittering chain around her mother's neck. Tharani wore a simple salwar kameez, but she had chosen a dark maroon one that set off the necklace and highlighted the stones. They shone and sparkled around her neck.

"It's Ramesh's. His mother's actually. A family heirloom apparently."

"He's given it to you?"

"No... not yet. He... .he felt it would look better on you."

Tharani's hands shook as she spoke and she put down her cup.

Yamini looked at her mother, then she blushed and looked at the floor. She was thoroughly flustered now and would have given anything to just not be there in that moment.

"No! No! I... I don't know how this happened!" She felt like she was suffocating, "He got the wrong idea."

Tharani nodded soothingly, and drank from her tea, "That's what I told him."

"What did he say?"

"He just nodded. Didn't say anything."

Yamini was calmer now, "Okay."

"I'll give back the necklace tomorrow."

"Okay. Please do."

Tharani got up to leave. "Ma?"

"Yes?"

"Did you even consider it? Did you consider...??"

"No. No, I didn't...till he told me that you liked him."

"Oh!!" Yamini was flustered all over again, "He knows! Oh God!" She buried her face in her hands.

Tharani reached out to her and patted her head, "It's okay honey. I'll take care of it and return the necklace. Maybe he shouldn't be around you girls so much."

She picked up the tea things and left. Yamini sat there, her eyes on her book but her mind elsewhere and racing. He had known! Of course he had known. She thought back to the moment their eyes had met in the mirror, and she cringed inwardly. "How could I have been that way?" Tears started from her eyes and flowed down her face. She did nothing to stop them or clear her face. She just let them flow. "There's no one here to guide me. I wish Appa..." Her thoughts trailed... "Who am I kidding? He's here because of Appa and Amma. He's here because he's paying my fees! Not my mom, not my dad, but a 25-year-old boyfriend of my mother is paying the fees. Oh God!!" Her shoulders shook as she cried. She buried her face in her hands and cried. She cried a long time. When she finally looked up, the sky was dark, with a sprinkling of stars. The streetlights were on. She picked up a towel nearby and wiped her face. Somehow she felt better for crying.

He'd be there for a while in their lives and then he'd move on. He'd marry, have kids, become a landlord... This was just fun time for him, sowing wild oats; and paying for the fun, of course. Throwing money at them from his surpluses. Did his mom value the necklace enough to know he had taken it or was it just another trinket? How much was it worth? Lakhs? Crores? She was too young to make a guess. "Perhaps enough to pay my college fees, since he is paying my fees anyways."

She looked into a house across the street. A man and woman were in the kitchen. They were talking and laughing as they moved around. They were apparently cooking together. The lady had on an apron. After a while, the man said something and the lady replied, and then he bent and picked her up and walked out the door even as she laughingly protested.

"Is that love?" Yamini mused, "Or was it just something that led to something else? A game. Is that how it all worked?"

"You dance around each other...some pins, a chart, two mirrors...a man and a woman. Aftershaves... shirt worn lightly over the shoulder...strong male hands, eyes meeting..."

Even as she watched a shooting star overhead, she felt a strong overwhelming emotion take over, and she knew what it was. Desire.

She got up gracefully to her feet and switched off the light in the balcony. She went into her mother's bedroom. Tharani was busy stitching on the sewing machine. "Would you like something to eat?" she asked Yamini, without looking up.

"No, not right now."

Yamini walked over the shelf and took out the slim jewellery box. She opened it and took out the necklace. She went over to the mirror, and standing in front of it, she placed the necklace around her neck and did the clasp. She stood there admiring herself, turning this way and that, so that the stones caught the light at various angles and sparkled.

Tharani looked up from her work and was startled. She gaped at the girl.

Yamini turned to her mother and smiled shyly, "It does look nice on me."

painted with dark clouds, too much too soon
give it time to grow... it's still New Moon

Ramesh knocked on the door and waited. It was Yamini who opened the door. She moved back to let him in. Tharani came out of the bedroom and closed the door. She came over to Ramesh. "You have to go," she said.

"What happened?" he asked, looking from Yamini to Tharani, a little alarmed.

Yamini blushed and left the room. "Sitara has come of age," said Tharani, matter-of-factly.

"Oh! That's good news!" he smiled. "Coming of age" was not a new term to him. It just meant that the girl had got her first period. In quite a few communities in South India—and indeed, in other places too through the rest of India—it is considered a life event and celebrated as a fact that the girl was now eligible for marriage. A function was generally held and relatives and friends were invited over to bless the girl. Before all that began, the girl would first be quarantined for five days to a week, given special food and beauty care and allowed to rest.

Ramesh was familiar with all this. He was from a village and was used to village customs and he had seen young girls in his own family go through it. And somehow, perhaps because of the rest and the beauty treatment with turmeric and other natural ingredients, the girl invariably glowed and seemed to grow up overnight. Mostly, after this, the girl would be treated as a young lady and not as a child anymore.

"Okay, I'll leave," he said. "Let me know if you need anything."

Tharani would have loved to hold a big function, but they did not know anyone, and those who knew her and her family did not want to associate with them. So, at the end of the seven days, she just called in Shanthi and she got the priest to come in too and perform the puja.

The gossip mills worked full time. By now, everyone in the neighbourhood knew what was going on. Association meetings had been held to discuss whether this family should be allowed to continue to live in the apartments. All rulings were stayed because there was no evidence, apart from the fact that Sushanth seemed to have no objection to Ramesh. The fact that Ramesh was the son of a Zamindar also weighed in. Surely the Zamindar would know how to control his son? They decided that it was now just a matter of time before he found out, and left it at that.

"This is such rubbish," said Sitara, as her mother broke an egg and poured the contents into her mouth. This was followed by a ladle full of gingelly oil. "What are these things supposed to do? They taste so yucky!"

"Stop fussing," said Tharani, "These things will strengthen your hip and help you during childbirth."

"Then I won't take them for sure. I'm not going to get married or have children."

"That's what you'll say now."

"Who will marry me? Daughter of a courtesan! Sister of a courtesan!"

Tharani did not answer, which somehow provoked Sitara to continue to taunt.

"No answer haan? Or maybe it's not marriage we're talking here. Maybe I'm just ready to be sold to the highest bidder? What would be my price? I won't settle for anything less than a house and a car and holidays."

"It's possible you will have to settle for much less," said Tharani, busily laying out the food on the plate.

Shocked silence seemed to stretch to eternity. Then a small voice said, "Ma? You wouldn't do that, would you?"

Tharani looked up into eyes so like her own. Huge gold flecked tawny eyes full of fire... Sitara's uncertain and terrified, and hers... .merciless.

"Eat your food."

And Tharani turned to leave. "Ma!"

But her mother was gone.

Tharani closed the door. "She is being difficult?" asked Shanthi.

"Very difficult. She knows too much."

"That's not good!"

Tharani looked at Shanthi seriously, "Actually, I think it's for the best. It's time she grew up. It's time she faced facts."

Shanthi looked at her wide-eyed. "Knowing is fine. But you wouldn't... you know... would you?"

"Why not?"

"Mother!"

Both of them turned to see Yamini standing in the hall. She had heard them talk. She looked furiously at her mother, "You will do no such thing! Leave Sitara alone! You can't do this!"

Tharani came into the hall, "Your father hasn't sent money these past two months. I haven't heard from him. Shanthi Aunty says they're investing in something and the money is going into that. But he hasn't called."

Yamini's lips trembled, "So go back to your tailoring job. I can work too. Just leave Sitara alone. Please!"

Tharani turned and looked at the statue that Ramesh had gifted her, now kept in a corner of the showcase. The artist had played with the senses. The white sari stuck to the body, showing tantalizing bits of brown here and there. It seemed like one could almost see the woman's nipples, and one tended to move the statue all around in the hope of being able to do so, but, well, they weren't visible.

She turned then to look straight into Yamini's eyes and said firmly, "Sitara is just like me. She will be alright."

And she turned and left for the kitchen.

It was well past nine when Sitara woke up. Her sisters had left for school, and they would be going to stay with Shanthi after school. She opened her eyes and looked out the window. A crow sat on a tree outside and cawed. She stared at it, yet unseeing, allowing the pain in her mind to grow to a proportion where tears rolled out her eyes and wet her pillow. She lay motionless, allowing them to flow. Time had become meaningless. Life had become meaningless. From this day on, anything and everything would be meaningless. Except death...

She reached over and pulled her mother's sari that was lying on the chair nearby and examined it. She turned and lay flat on her back and stared at the ceiling fan. She was crying in earnest now. "This makes sense. Only this makes sense now. The ceiling fan and mother's sari as a rope... By the end of the day for sure! Maybe now is the right time, before anything happens..."

Tharani walked into the room and over to her. She saw the tears. She sat down on the bed and bent her head in deep thought. Then she looked up, "Okay."

Sitara looked at her. "What do you mean, "okay?"

"You need not do it. We'll manage somehow."

And suddenly the tigress pounced, "Ohhhhh!! So gracious! Tharani the Gracious!! She can concede defeat with grace! Now you can go and tell Shanthi Aunty, "I did not do it. I resisted. I needed money but I resisted." And Shanthi Aunty will say, "I'm glad you did. She's too young for this." Isn't that what she'll say? That I'm too young for this? Not "thank God you decided not to. Let her go. Never do this to her again!" Just "too young for this." Isn't that what she'll say?"

"I don't want your stupid charity!" she continued, "I'm not that special that you should spare me. You didn't spare yourself. You didn't spare Yamini. So why should you spare me? But listen!" she clutched Tharani's blouse fiercely and pulled her close, "If you take one step towards Sheila, I swear by every God I worship and by every spell that you have ever cast that I'll kill you, and then, I'll kill myself."

Tharani did not flinch. She just stared stolidly back at Sitara, her face a wooden mask, "I promise."

Sitare let go of her blouse, "So stop trying to be noble when you don't know what noble means. Help me get through this."

Tharani nodded, then turned and left the room.

The day passed slowly and gradually. Soon, it was time. She stood by the door next to her mother, barefoot, a head taller than her, a graceful, slim, beautiful figure clad in a white chiffon long skirt that flowed to the floor with a matching pure white short blouse. Except for a pat of talcum powder, she wore no other makeup and no ornaments. Her kohl-marked eyes were big and wide. She wore no scent.

Her mother took her by the arm, led her into the room, and closed the door firmly, locking it from outside. She heard the click and lowered her head.

"Amma!" she cried, the one last frantic terror-filled cry of a dying person, and then her voice trailed... It was a child that had entered the room filled with fear, but it was a woman's eyes that lifted and surveyed the room, taking in the bed with its velvet covers scattered with red rose petals, the candles that burned here and there, throwing dancing shadows, her own reflection in the mirror across, showing a stranger in white, a beautiful sensuous girl she had never met before. There were no tears as she walked across and threw off the covers on the bed. Some more rose petals. "Why would someone want to make love to a dead body?" Why?" And then, the tears came flowing down, crying for what was lost forever. But she wiped her face hurriedly with the back of her hand, composed herself, and sat down on the floor, raising her knees so her skirt spread around her, and she hugged her knees and sat there waiting.

The door opened and he came in. He shut the door, and turned to look at her. Their eyes met, and he backed towards the wall, away from her. He looked across the room at her, never once moving his eyes away. He saw fear and anger in those tawny golden eyes. They burned with hatred and fierce anger. They dared him to come closer. His mind wavered and his eyes flickered with uncertainty. Did he really want this? And then, his mind went back to his encounters with her mother and her sister, and he knew for sure then that it would alright. This was a courtesan: a natural in the art of lovemaking; yet to bloom...

And he was a courtesan too, a man who knew what a woman wanted, sometimes better than she herself did.

He smiled at her and noted the flicker of confusion in hers. He moved over to the cot and sat on the edge, her side, just above her.

He looked down at her and said gently, "Do you not want this?"

She looked up at him, "I have my whole life to live."

He was listening to her intently, "Your life will be there."

"Why are you doing this?"

"There can only be one reason."

Her eyes grew wide in disbelief. "You desire me?"

"Yes."

"Just like you "desired" my mother and my sister?"

He did not flinch. "Is that wrong? Do you not desire me?"

She looked at him then, sitting there, young and handsome...and weak, and was filled with hatred so overwhelming that it consumed her.

"NO!!!"

"Touch me," he said.

"NO!"

He leaned over and touched her cheek, and trailed his hand over to her lips. She cringed away from his hand.

"Listen, Sitara, I will not do anything if you don't want me to. We...we can just pretend something happened, and then go out there. Don't think or feel like you don't have a choice. You do."

She looked at him, wide-eyed, "Really? I have choices? So why did you do this in the first place? Why are we here if all you wanted to do was give me choices? Why not just leave me alone?"

He shook his head, "I desire you. Have no doubts about that. But I can't be with a woman against her will. I...I don't want it that way."

"Huh! So you have a conscience! You have principles! The woman must consent! I am a child. I'm 13. You shouldn't even be here!"

He sighed, "Okay, if that's how you feel."

He got up to go.

"Wait."

He turned towards her. She blushed, "How much...how much....??"

"I gave your mother a gold necklace and a couple of gold bangles, a total worth of three lakhs."

Her eyes widened, "And you will take it back now?"

He looked at her and his eyes softened, "No, I won't."

Sitara looked at him and suddenly remembered Yamini's words, "It could have been worse..."

"Don't go out yet. Sit and talk to me,"

He came back and sat on the bed, same as before, just above her.

He was speaking, "Yes? You want something from me..."

"I...Will you be gentle?"

"I don't know otherwise, Sitara," his hand was on her face and he caressed her cheek with his thumb, "You want something from me. And I want something from you."

She would not lift her eyes.

"Come here," he said, gently, "And holding her hands, he helped her to her feet and sat her next to him.

"You look beautiful tonight."

"You would know, wouldn't you?"

He smiled.

"I fell down from my bike while coming here. There's a bruise."

"Oh!" she said, "Where?"

He lifted his shirt a little and showed her the angry red bruise on his waist.

"Have you applied anything?"

"I will. It's not hurting so much now. It did though."

She reached out a hand to tentatively touch the bruise. "Ouch!" he cried.

She smiled into his eyes and said with a return of some of her arrogance, "I am glad you hurt. You deserve it."

He looked deeply into her eyes and he wasn't smiling back. His eyes were filled with desire. He raised his eyes to take in her hair, taking in their glossiness, then moved slowly to her ears, her cheek, her nose, her mouth…lingering there before looking deeply into her eyes again. He gently put his hand on her arm. She was a young and healthy girl and her body had been readied to expect love since that morning, but her mind had held back. But now, she looked back at him, mesmerized. She could not take her eyes off of his. Pinpoint sensations of pleasure awakened in her wherever he touched and she felt a strange pain in the pit of her stomach that was far from unpleasant. Ramesh did nothing to step up the pace. He continued to look into her eyes, continued to show her how much he desired her, knowing full well that with the slightest of wrong gestures, she would take flight like a frightened young colt. And all of a sudden, the fear in her was gone. There was nothing to fear here. This was an old friend who knew her well. He was gentle, always had been.

She did not stop his hand as he pushed back her hair, even while tracing a line down to her lips and lingering there. He bent his head and his lips barely touched hers, and she felt his hot breath in her mouth. The male scent of his body engulfed her and she felt drunk with desire. He moved his head back to look intensely into her beautiful golden eyes. They looked back at him then, mesmerized, burning now with desire. His own were searching, seeking to understand her needs, allowing her take the lead... She reached out and wound her arms around his neck and pulled him close, till their lips locked and they fell back on the bed together.

The candles burned merrily on...

CHAPTER 8

Someone sang a country song, someone played a tune
How soothing is the moonlight, how beautiful is the moon!

Was he intimidating because he was so tall and huge or because he was Rudrayunsh, the Zamindar of Rasapalayam? But the truth was that he was a gentle, fun-loving man with a good sense of justice. He was a family man who loved his wife and children very much. He was also considered a very good landlord by all those who came under his jurisdiction. The zamindari system has been abolished in India, but his family still retained some personal property. He had wisely aligned himself with the political parties of his times, being a neutral player and only interested in the social upliftment of his people. The payoff from this was that he still wielded quite some power. He was well known in the surrounding villages, as are most aristocratic families, and he was treated with immense respect and love wherever he went.

He now sat in the big wooden swing in his huge living room. It was a misnomer to call it a living room. It was so big it was more of a hall that could accommodate a hundred or more people at a time. This was his house, this beautiful, palatial building of marble and stone, the house where he had grown up, the house that his children grew up in, and the house that would be passed on to his grandchildren as their homestead too.

The swing was a big wooden plank made of teakwood, and it was suspended from the ceiling by four strong iron chains. It was right in the middle of the hall. Adjacent to the hall was the dining room.

He swung himself to and fro gently, lost deep in thought. Then he came to a decision. He called out, "Mohan!" Only, his voice was so deep that it sounded like a Boom! His shout made his wife, Savitri, who was in the kitchen adjacent to the hall, drop the vessel that she was holding. They had been married 40 years now, but even then, she had not got used to his booming voice. She glared at him from the kitchen, having retrieved the vessel. "Why are you shouting?"

He turned to her, "Arrey! I'm not shouting. I am calling."

She turned back to the stove, "One of these days, you'll lose your voice. Then you'll be squeaking like a mouse. Squeak! Squeak!"

Rudra looked affectionately towards the kitchen, "You'll be there to make me a warm concoction should that happen."

"Ai, a very bitter tasting one," she chuckled back.

Meanwhile, the odd-job man named Mohan had come in. He alternated as the chief gardener as well. He was standing deferentially, with his hands folded, waiting for his master to speak.

"Mohan, how's the garden work coming along?"

"Very well, Sir. I've just planted some hybrid variety of coconut trees. They are short but the yield is very good."

"Glad to hear that. Mohan, you live in the village on the other side, don't you?"

"Yes Sir."

"Your village is very big."

"Yes Sir. But it's still quite remote and unreachable. The roads are not good Sir."

"Is that so?"

"Yes Sir. There is no road Sir. Just a mud track where the bushes have been cleared up."

"I must look into that."

"Yes Sir. Thank you Sir."

"I believe the headmaster of the village school lives there? I have heard of him though I haven't met him yet."

"Yes Sir, he does. He and his daughter Devika run the school.

"Ah, yes, Devika, his daughter. How old is she?"

"I have known her since she was born. She must be about 20 now, the same age as my daughter."

"Good, good. Is she getting married?"

"No Sir, not that I know of. They are poor people Sir. She has no mother. Her mother died when she was a baby. Her father brought her up single-handedly. The women who live near them—even my wife—they took care of the baby. Very good girl, Sir, if I may say so. Very respectful. She's well educated. Went to college in the city. She has completed her degree. That's why she's able to help her father."

"I've heard that she is very beautiful."

"Yes Sir! She is."

Rudra swung to and fro thoughtfully. Then he looked up and said, "You may go, Mohan. Thank you."

After Mohan had gone, Rudra called a number, "Khalil, could you come over?"

Savitri, who had been too busy in the kitchen to hear any of the conversation between her husband and Mohan, now came out of the kitchen and said, "Breakfast is ready. Please come to the table."

Rudra nodded and got off the swing and went over to wash his hands. He was still eating his breakfast when Khalil arrived. Khalil was the supervisor that Rudra had appointed to check on Ramesh. He was Rudra's bosom friend and trusted right-hand man. Rudra and Khalil had grown up together, studied in the same class and been to the same college. Khalil stood in no ceremony with Rudra and was considered a member of the family. He came up to the table and sat down in a chair adjacent to Rudra's chair.

"Have you eaten?" asked Savitri.

"Yes, Akka, I have. They won't allow me to step out without eating."

Savitri smiled. By "they," he meant his family: his wife and three children.

"How are the children?"

He threw up his hands in mock despair, "Please don't even ask! It's holidays and they're ripping the house apart. Oooofff!! Running here and there, jumping up and down! It feels crazy!"

Savitri laughed and Rudra smiled, "They are children. This is the time to enjoy life. Just look at us! All the time worrying about something or the other."

Savitri looked sharply at her husband, wondering what was worrying him. She was attuned to his body language and she knew that he was deeply troubled. However, she did not say anything.

Khalil had also looked sharply at him.

"You wanted to talk to me?"

"Yes Khalil, that's why I called you."

Rudra finished his meal and got up to wash his hands. He then picked up the coffee that his wife had placed on the table. Khalil picked up his cup too, and they moved back to the swing. Rudra once again sat on the swing and Khalil pulled up a chair nearby and sat down.

"Please tell me what's bothering you."

Rudra turned to his wife, "Savitri, I need you to come and join this conversation."

She nodded and stopped clearing up the table, washed her hands, and came and sat down on the swing, next to him.

"Isn't there something you should be telling me?" Rudra asked Khalil.

Khalil squirmed uneasily in his seat, "Maybe."

"I put you in charge of my son. Then I took you out of it. Did that tell you that your duty towards this family is over?"

"No, no! It was not like that! How can that be? I was out of station, you know that! I've only been back a week now." Then he lowered his head, "But when I came back, I heard... there were rumours..."

He looked up, "So I checked. I needed proof before I came to you. I didn't want you saying that I was making false accusations against your son."

"And?"

"And, well, now I have proof."

Khalil searched in his phone and found the video he was looking for, and showed it to Rudra. Both Rudra and Savitri watched it. It showed Ramesh getting off his bike and going into the apartment building where Tharani and her family lived.

"Is it possible he is innocent?"

"The lady is well known to be a fleecer. I had warned him about her."

"He did not listen?"

Khalil shrugged, "She is extremely manipulative. You know how it is."

Rudra nodded. Savitri turned to him angrily, "How do you know how it is?"

He looked at his wife, "Arrey! I'm a Zamindar. I deal with such cases."

He winked at Khalil and said slyly to her, "What did you think it was?"

She shook her head haughtily, "Never mind what I thought. This is about our son. Continue."

"But I thought you said…"

"Never mind what I said. Continue!"

Rudra turned to Khalil and said seriously, "This has got to stop right now."

Khalil nodded.

"Can they…can she be bought off?"

Khalil shook his head, "I'm not sure. The previous person was fleeced to death... literally."

"Oh!" Rudra thought for a while, and then he shrugged, "That leaves me with only one other option: to speak to my son and get him to see reason….and to agree to get married. It is high time he got married."

Both Khalil and Savitri looked at him in surprise. Whatever else it was that they had expected him to say, it was certainly not this. While Khalil remained silent, Savitri asked, "But who will marry a boy like that? True, he is a Zamindar's son, but which girl will want an unfaithful husband? Even I will not wish such a boy on my own daughter."

"I was speaking to Mohan today morning," said Rudra, "He said that the village schoolmaster has a beautiful daughter named Devika. They are good people. She is well educated, intelligent, respectful, and from a good family. But they are poor."

Khalil's eyes widened and so did Savitri's. "Don't you think that you're making a mistake?" asked Khalil, "You're talking about a girl's life here."

"No, I'm not making a mistake."

"The girl also has a dosha (discrepancy) in her horoscope," added Khalil.

"All the better!" said Rudra, enthusiastically.

This time, both of them said simultaneously, "How is it 'all the better'?"

"They will at least consider the possibility of a marriage, while others won't do even that," explained Rudra.

They were both silent and looked mutinous. So he continued,

"Look, my son has made a mistake... is making a mistake. And I feel marriage will set him right. After the marriage, I will hand over the running of the estate to him. With the huge responsibility he won't be able to play around all that much. He will sober up. But for that, I need a nice girl. She must be from a good family. I'm not very particular about her caste or horoscope. I don't believe in all that. I'm willing to overlook somethings in this girl, and in return…"

"No!" said Savitri, firmly. They both looked at her. "I know Devika. She comes to the temple and we get along very well. She's a very good girl: very respectful and extremely beautiful and talented. She is poor, but so what? Doesn't she deserve someone better? I know I'm speaking about my son, and I love him very much, but I would not wish him on her."

"But the decision will be hers," Rudra pointed out, "I'm not going to deceive them. I'm going to tell them everything, and then, let them decide."

"But you're still being manipulative. You're taking advantage of their situation in life."

"Yes, I am being manipulative. I'm going to them only because I feel they'll consider the alliance. Is that being manipulative? Yes. But they will know that! They will know that I'm being manipulative. And they will also know that I am a beggar... begging for my son to be given a chance…"

His voice shook, and Savitri put a hand on his shoulder to steady him.

Khalil asked, "Shall I come with you?"

"No, you go. You have a lot of work to do. But stop being selfish and take care of my work too."

Khalil glared at him, "When have I... ?" Then he saw the grin on Rudra's face, "Oh please! Seriously Akka, how do you put up with him?"

Savitri said shortly, "I don't."

The men laughed at that. "Well, I'll be on my way. If you want anything done, shout out. Good luck!"

After he left, the couple were silent for a while. Then Savitri said, "I have something to tell you."

Rudra looked at her.

She hesitated, "I... my jewels are missing."

Rudra raised his brow, "What do you mean missing?"

"My gold jewellery, some of them are missing. Two necklaces and some bangles."

"You're telling me now?!! Why is everyone being so deceptive?"

Savitri looked angrily at him, "Well, I found out only today morning as I was checking out what to wear to the wedding reception today evening. And why should I be afraid of you, pray? You may be Zamindar of Rasapalayam, but to me you're... .you're my husband!"

"And that doesn't scare you?"

"No. Oh! Stop provoking me and talk about our son."

"Well, I'm going right now to meet the girl and her father."

"Do you think that's right?" asked Savitri, doubtfully.

"We'll never know till we've asked."

"What if they get angry and tell everyone?"

"Everyone will either know my son is a wastrel puppy or that his father is a master manipulator. How does it matter in a flood how much water goes over your head? It's a flood!"

"Hmmm..."

"What are you hmmming about? You did a bad job bringing up that boy!"

Savitri got up from the swing and looked deeply into Rudra's eyes, "Well, I did my best. But guess what? He turned out to be just like his father!"

And she walked away, nose in air, leaving Rudra spluttering with rage.

In earlier days, an emissary would first be sent to announce the arrival of the landlord or king, but in modern times... Rudra, the Zamindar, sat in his car and stared out.

"It's a mud track Sir. Can't go there by car."

"I can see that. I suppose I will have to get out and walk. How far is it to the village?"

"Two kilometres, Sir."

"Two kilometres in the hot Sun! Are you kidding me?"

"No Sir. That's the only way to get there."

"I need to do something about this. Why haven't I got a road laid here yet?"

All the same, he got out and opened his umbrella.

"Should I wait here, Sir?"

Rudra looked at his driver, "I saw a pub a little way off. Stay there. I'll be back."

"Okay Sir."

Half-an-hour later, Rudra arrived at the village, hot and tired. He called to a lady passing by with a pot of water, "Where's the schoolmaster's house?"

"Schoolmaster? That one!"

She pointed to a gate and what looked like a lush garden behind it. The house wasn't visible at all.

"Inside that gate?"

"Yes."

"Thank you."

He went over and opened the gate and went it.

It was a beautiful garden with flower bushes and trees. The house was a tiny cottage nestled within. A man sat in the porch, reading a newspaper. He was tiny and skinny old man, rather nondescript, with grey hair and a wrinkled face. He had on spectacles. But he also looked dignified and strict. Very much the village schoolmaster.

He looked up when Rudra walked in. "Who is it?"

Rudra went up to him, "I'm Rudra, Zamindar of Rasapalayam."

"Oh! Oh my God! Please come in! Devika! Please come in Sir." The man looked flustered.

Rudra removed his slippers and followed the man into the living room. It was a bright and airy room, very tastefully decorated. The schoolmaster said, "Please sit down."

Rudra chose a comfortable chair and settled down.

The inherent Indian hospitality prevailed, "Will you have something to eat Sir?"

"No, no, I just had my breakfast. But a glass of water will be very welcome."

"Sure. Devika!"

Rudra heard the pleasant tinkling sound of anklets, and then a girl appeared from inside the house. Rudra stared at her. He couldn't help it. She was so beautiful! She was fair and slim... a little over five feet three inches maybe. Her face was radiant and glowing, with perfect features. Her eyes were a strange shade of blue-green. She wore a plain light pink sari in the traditional way. There was goodness in the face... and innocence. Rudra found that strange that in that age and time that a girl could look innocent.

"Devika, this is the Zamindar of Rasapalayam."

Devika folded her hands in namaste. "Please could you bring him some water? He's come from afar. Also, if you could make some coffee?"

"Sure Appa."

The girl smiled at Rudra and turned and went in.

"Please sit down," said Rudra to the schoolmaster.

The man continued to stand, unwilling to be on equal terms with the Zamindar.

"Is there anything I can do for you?"

"Well, actually, I came to talk to both you and your daughter. So we'll wait till she is here."

Devika came in with the water and gave it to Rudra. "Child, the coffee can wait. Will you please sit down? I have come a long way just to talk to you."

She nodded, and unlike her father, had no qualms in occupying the chair next to Rudra. He could not take his eyes off her face.

He drank the water and placed the glass on the table, "I came here to ask you something."

She did not say anything, but she was watching him carefully, her head tilted to one side.

Rudra looked at the man standing with folded hands, "Sir, you need to sit down. Please do take a seat."

The schoolmaster reluctantly sat down opposite Rudra.

"I... I have heard a lot about you," said Rudra to Devika, "I have heard that you are beautiful and very intelligent and well educated. I have heard that you're a teacher and that you help your father run the school."

She nodded, "Yes Sir."

"I appreciate that. Without people like you and your father, our children would not be able to dream of a life outside of these villages."

Devika smiled, as did her father, "Thank you Uncle. We try our best to keep things going."

"Yes, I can see that. And now that I know how far this village is and how remote, I will certainly help out."

"Thank you Uncle," said Devika, once more.

Rudra looked at his hands, "But that's not what I've come here to talk to you about."

They were silent, waiting for him to continue.

Rudra continued to look at his hands, "I... I have a son, as you know...or probably don't."

"I do know," Devika interrupted, unexpectedly, "I had lost my way in the fair when I was 10 years old. He brought me back home."

"Oh!" said Rudra, "So you have met him... a long time back?"

"Yes. I have seen him several times after that...on my way to school...then college. He would pass by on his bike...sometimes with his friends."

Something in her voice made Rudra look at her, startled. There was animation in that voice.

"He must have been a teenager when he helped you in the fair."

"Yes."

"I remember him telling us that he had helped a little girl who was lost. So that was you?"

"Yes."

"Ah! So, yes, you know I have a son. His name is Ramesh. He went to college. He's completed his engineering. He is now 26 years old. We have a lot of property. We have fields. Rice fields. So we have shops to sell the rice. And I had put Ramesh in charge of one of these shops in the city. So, one day, a lady came to buy rice in that shop..."

He stopped and looked up at her, "She was not a nice lady... you understand?"

She looked uncertainly at him, then at her father. His face was expressionless. So she turned back to Rudra and nodded uncertainly.

"My son... he is caught by this lady... enamoured is the right word. She...she has him under her spell. She is old enough to be his mother. I...I want to save my son. I want him to get back to the right path. Otherwise I will lose him. I also have a daughter, Meenakshi. She is to be married soon. Her life will be spoilt too."

He was silent again. Devika looked at her father. His face had become very wooden now, completely devoid of expression. Years of living with him told her that he was livid with rage.

"I... I want to ask if you will marry my son." It was out now. There was nothing he could do to retract his words. "I know what I'm asking is wrong, but..."

"But you heard that we're poor and that my daughter has a dosha in her horoscope and so you thought that you could manipulate us into accepting your useless son?" said the schoolmaster, getting up and glaring at Rudra, although in his heart, he was very afraid.

Rudra grew red with anger but he controlled himself and said politely, "You can say no, but don't call my son useless. I am a father just like you. I would not come to you if my son was a bad boy. He is not! He is just misled."

"Well, then, the answer is no."

Rudra's shoulders sagged in defeat, "Okay. Okay, I understand that. But I want you to understand that I... I won't deny that I was trying to take advantage of your...situation. But I also want you to remember that I overlooked everything. Horoscope does not bother me neither does your poverty. But I did want a girl from a good family, that's all. And I also want you to remember that I did not come to you in arrogance. I came to you humbly, with a request."

"Would you ask a rich girl with a good horoscope to marry your son?"

"Under normal circumstances, yes. But now, no...they will not agree."

"You have considered my daughter to be low...so low, so irredeemable that she will accept anyone who offers for her. We may be poor people, Sir, but we have our dignity."

"Yes... I suppose that's how it appears," Rudra got up, "I'm sorry. I did not mean to hurt either of you. Particularly you," he said to Devika, "You certainly are a remarkable girl and very beautiful, if I may say so. In fact, the most beautiful girl I have ever seen. My wife, Savitri, says she meets you in the temple and that you are a very good girl. She seems to like you a lot." He placed a hand on her head, "God Bless you child. You will make any man proud to be your husband."

He turned to the schoolmaster and folded his hands, "Forgive me if you can."

And he took leave.

There was silence after he had gone. The schoolmaster glared at the door through which he had gone, "The nerve of him! Coming to my house and insulting me!"

Devika looked up at her father and said, "I want to marry Ramesh."

Her father turned and gaped at her, stupefied. "What?" he said, thinking he had not heard right, "What did you say?"

"I said I want to marry Ramesh."

"Are you out of your mind?? Have you gone crazy?? Didn't you hear the man?"

"Yes I did. That's why I'm saying I want to marry Ramesh."

"What do you mean by that's why?"

"Appa, the man has a problem. His son has gone astray."

"That's their business, not ours."

"It's their only chance Appa."

Her father moved here and there, agitated, "You're crazy! The boy has slept with a woman. He's possibly slept with so many other women. He's a zamindar's son. Did they come to us when he was okay? Oh! Why am I even trying to explain? This is just not happening."

"Okay, Appa. If you don't want it, it's definitely not happening. But... I just happen to like Ramesh."

"Like? You don't even know him."

"I liked him when he rescued me."

"You were 10 years old."

"Yes... and he bought me this chain. I still have it with me. He put it around my neck and he said, "And now, we're married. You're my wife." Then he laughed and left with his friends."

"And so you think you are his wife?"

"No...not because of that. I just think it strange how he keeps walking into my life..."

"So you think you're both meant to be."

"Yes. I... I really liked him then. And I've seen him quite often, you know. On my way to school...with my friends. He's very handsome."

Her father stared at her.

"I really like him Appa."

"Then you have to bury your liking. Because I will definitely not consent to this recklessness and give my only daughter, who is as pure as snow, to a wastrel."

"Okay Appa."

Devika got up and took the glass that Rudra had placed on the table and went into the kitchen.

The schoolmaster collapsed in his chair, suddenly feeling very tired and drained out. Things had happened too suddenly and he wasn't well enough to cope with them. As it turned out, his consent wasn't going to be necessary after all. When Devika woke up in the morning and found that her father was still asleep, she became alarmed. She tried to wake him up, but he wouldn't. She then called the village doctor, who came in, checked the pulse, and declared him dead.

When Rudra heard about the death of the schoolmaster, he was stricken with guilt. "Oh my God! What have I done?" he said to his wife, Savitri.

She tried to console him, "Please, this is not your fault. You did not expect this to happen. I am sure you were polite. I am sure you did not hurt him."

"But... my being there, asking him, that in itself was an insult. How could I do that?"

"You... you were not thinking. You were worried about your son. He was a father too. I am sure he forgave you."

Khalil walked in. "Khalil, see what I've done! I've killed a man!" said Rudra, dramatically.

Khalil snorted. "What did you do? The man was old, he died. He's been ailing for a while now. You just put the lid on it."

"Really? Was he that ill?"

"Yes. Diabetes, high blood pressure, already had two strokes. He was on his way out. And, by the way, you think you're so powerful you can kill people with your words, is it?"

"Khalil, I believe so, going by the result."

"Well, you're not. You're just an ordinary old Zamindar who went begging. So shut up."

Thus put in his place, Rudra did shut up. He and his wife went to the schoolmaster's house to offer their condolences and offer Devika all the help that she needed. The funeral took place in the afternoon.

"Savitri, you go back home. I'll stay here and see if I can be of any further help," Rudra told his wife, "The child is alone, poor thing."

She nodded and left for home soon after. Rudra stayed on, making arrangements for the memorial function the next day. He also enquired from her lawyer, Devika's financial status, to see if he could help her in any way. He didn't get a chance to speak to her. She was too heartbroken and was crying. And later, she became involved in the funeral arrangements.

Rudra came back the next day for the memorial function and partook in the meal. And although almost everyone left soon after, he stayed on to see if he could get a chance to speak to her alone. There was something he needed to update her about. He had decided to help her financially and also to ensure she was able to hold her job as school teacher with a comfortable salary. At no point did it occur to him to renew his request for her to marry Ramesh. As far as he was concerned, that was over. Her father had spoken and the decision was final. What he now felt was compassion and a certain amount of responsibility for her welfare.

It was then evening. The day had been a cloudy one, and now, a soft, cold wind blew through the garden, rustling the trees.

"Hi Uncle," said a voice as he stood there in the garden, looking up at the darkened sky so full of clouds.

He turned around and saw Devika standing there.

"Hi child."

"It's going to rain."

"Yes. I should be going before it does."

"Yes, I think you should. The track gets very muddy when it rains."

"I must see that the road is laid soon," said Rudra.

He looked at her, "Devika, I'm sorry about your father. I hope... I hope it was not my coming to your house that..."

"Oh no, Uncle. Appa had been unwell for a long time. He was upset, yes. But he had made up his mind, so I don't think he was too troubled."

Rudra nodded, "I'm glad to hear that."

And then, because she was a simple and innocent young girl, "Uncle, I would like to marry your son."

Rudra's reaction was so like her father's. The same stupified stare, and then, "What?"

She waited for him to comprehend what she had just said, but he just repeated, "What? What's that you're saying?"

"I mean it. I want to marry your son."

Rudra shook his head, "You don't know what you're saying. You're still in shock."

"I told my father that I wanted to marry him."

Rudra looked startled, "But why did you tell him that?"

"Because that's what I want."

"And why do you want to marry my son?"

She was blushing now, but she continued, "I... . he bought me a chain at the fair, and when he brought me home, he put that chain around my neck and he said, "now we're married. You're my wife"."

Rudra struggled to grasp this, "Okay... but you were very young then. It meant nothing."

"No, not to him."

"So..ah! It meant something to you! Is that what you're trying to say?"

"Yes."

"You fell in love with him?"

"Yes."

"But you haven't seen him since then."

"I have. On my way to school... to college. He would go by on his bike... sometimes with his friends... sometimes alone."

"Did he recognize you?"

"No. He never turned in my direction."

"Ah! But you saw him and liked him."

"Yes."

"But then, your father said no."

"My father is not here now. I will have to take a lot of decisions on my own."

"And this is your decision? To marry my son?"

"Yes."

"Are you sure that's the only reason you want to marry my son? What if it's because you're broke and also afraid to live by yourself? What if you're afraid you will never get married?"

She looked at him straight in the face, "Yes, what if I was? What then? How does it matter what my reasons are?"

Rudra gaped at the girl, so young and slim, standing up to him so boldly, and he knew then a moment of sheer rage. How dare this impudent girl talk to him like that! Talk like that to the Zamindar of Rasapalayam! But then, he cooled down and looked at her beautiful innocent face and laughed, "You're a very bold person. No one has spoken to me like that."

"And no one has spoken to me like that either," she said, simply.

He nodded, agreeing. If he could manipulate, so could she. Fair enough.

"Very well. What if my son doesn't come back to you? What if you are destroying your own life completely?"

"At least I would have married the man I love."

Rudra believed in her then. This was no gold digger. This was a young girl deeply in love.

"Come here child."

She went over to him. He looked deep into her eyes. He then placed a hand on her head and said, "Thank you."

Her lips trembled and a teardrop rolled down her cheek, "I... I must go in... Appa."

And she ran into the house.

A sudden gush of cold breeze swept around the Zamindar as he stood there, and then, a drop of rain fell on his head, followed by another, and another. He looked up at the sky and he could see the raindrops by the street light. He raised both hands to the sky and said, "Everything will be alright. Thank you Father!"

CHAPTER 9

There's so much going on below,
Oh my! Dear Me!
Said the Moon, overwhelmed,
"What all I have to see!"

Meanwhile, all was not well at the Tharani-Sushanth homestead, if it could be called that.

"So," said Sitara, conversationally, sitting on the kitchen counter, "We have the same boyfriend. You—my mamma—and I. How does he treat you?"

Tharani coloured and didn't answer. She pretended to stir the curry. "Does he rub your back? Or does he... ?? You know..." She looked teasingly at her mother, "Because he likes to rub my back with... you know!"

"Sitara!" called Yamini, from the doorway, "Come and help me with this."

Sitara got off the counter and made her way to her sister, "Yo! Yamini to the rescue!"

She went with Yamini to the bedroom and helped her lift the bed on to the cot. Yamini had been cleaning up and dusting her bed.

"Sitara," said Yamini, quietly, "Spare her."

"No, I won't," said Sitara, shaking her head from side to side, her curls moving too, "Why should I after what she's done to me? She's sold me, she's sold you. You want to call her 'mother,' that's your call. I'd like to rename her 'Pimp' or 'Whore'."

"Shut up, Sitara! You're just making things worse."

"Am I?" said Sitara, throwing down the mattress and moving belligerently towards Yamini, "Am I the one who's creating the trouble? Did I ask for this? Ask her to give my childhood back! Can she? Can she??!!"

She was hysterical, and she pinned Yamini to the wall. Tharani opened the door and came in. She grabbed Sitara by the shoulders, "Sitara, please come with me."

Sitara shrugged her arms off angrily. "Don't touch me! You make me sick!"

And she stalked out of the room.

Yamini and Tharani stared at each other. Tharani could see the pain and terror in the girl's face. Yamini's lips were trembling and her hands crossed her chest. And then, CRASH!! The sound came from the hall. They ran into the hall and found that Sitara had overturned the table and everything in it. Crockery and dishes and spoons and books and other paraphernalia lay on the floor, scattered. The table had toppled to one side and lay like a man shot dead. A few chairs had been shot dead too and lay on their backs, their feet up in the air. And Sitara was seated on the sofa looking defiantly at her mother. Tharani took a step forward, then checked herself, warned by the pure hatred in the girl's eyes. "Give me my food," she ordered. Tharani went into the kitchen, took out a plate, placed a couple of idlis in it and some chatni, and brought it over to Sitara. She took the plate from her mother. She seemed to have quietened down. Tharani turn to go back to the kitchen. CRASH!! The plate was flung across the hall and landed at the petrified Yamini's feet. Sitara got up and went into the bedroom and locked herself.

Tharani, who had run out of the kitchen at the noise, looked at the food on the floor. She turned to Yamini, "Go and get dressed and leave for school. I'll take care of this."

Yamini nodded. But even as she turned to go, the bedroom door opened and Sitara came out with her clothes and towel, went into the bathroom, and shut the door.

"Go to the other bathroom and have your bath," said Tharani to Yamini. She nodded and went into her bedroom.

Sitara came out in her uniform, went into the bedroom and shut the door. Soon she was out, dressed, hair combed, and her bag ready. She went and sat on the sofa and waited for Yamini. Yamini was soon ready too.

"Have some breakfast," Tharani coaxed Yamini. She shook her head and said, "No, we're late."

Sitara walked out the door and Yamini followed. Tharani watched out of the window as the girls made their way to the bus stop. Thankfully, Sheila studied in a different school and had left earlier. The child was too young and she was indeed protected well from whatever was going on.

Tharani sighed and turned to go in. She took in the mess. The food splashed across the floor and on to the walls. Mess and chaos everywhere. She sighed... . And slowly, and feeling very tired all of a sudden, she set about cleaning up.

It took her a couple of hours to set the house right, but it was finally done. The dishes had been washed, the clothes hung, everything set in its place. She made herself a cup of tea and sat down by the side table where the landline phone was, and she dialled out Shanthi's number.

"Hello!"

"Tharani, hi! How are you?"

"Not so well, Shanthi," and she proceeded to tell her about her woes.

"Relax. She is young and wild. She will temper down by and by."

"Yes... Shanthi, I haven't heard from Sushanth in quite a while now. It's been two months..."

"Oh..."

Something in her voice made Tharani sit up, "What is it?"

"Nothing."

"Shanthi, if there's something I should know..."

She heard a sigh. "Yes. Yes, there is. Sushanth... .he, well, likes a woman."

"What do you mean "likes a woman"?"

"He's been living with this woman. She joined the store as cashier."

"He's having an affair with her?"

"Yes... he stays at her place. She's middle-aged and a widow. She and her brother share an apartment."

"And Sushanth stays with them?"

"Yes. Yes, he does."

Tharani's heart went cold. She was silent, trying to process the information.

"Tharani?"

"I'll... I'll call you later. I need to think."

"Yes. Okay. I understand."

And Shanthi rang off. Tharani sat there, feeling numb. Her mind was not really working. What... .How?? Where do they go from here?

Suddenly, the phone rang. She picked up the receiver automatically, "Yes?"

"Madam, is this Mrs. Tharani?"

"Yes."

"I'm the Correspondent from the school, Ma'am. Your two girls study here. Sitara and Yamini."

"Yes," said Tharani, her heart going icy cold, "Is there something the matter? Are they okay?"

The Correspondent's voice sounded uncertain, "Yes, Ma'am, they're okay. But we have had some trouble from one of them. Sitara... The Principal wants you to come over immediately. Could you please come in right now?"

Tharani relaxed. The girls were physically okay. Sitara, of course! She had acted up.

"Yes, I'll come immediately."

She then called Shanthi. "Shanthi, I have to go to the school. Sitara..."

"I'll come over right now. We'll go together."

"Thank you Shanthi."

She placed the receiver, and went and got ready.

At the school, they made their way to the Principal's office and were shown in. The Principal, Mrs. Lalitha Shankar, looked up. She was a middle-aged lady, beautifully but simply dressed, very dignified—every inch the Principal of a prestigious school. She wore a crisp cotton sari and her hair was coiffured elegantly. She looked up from the papers she had been signing and gestured to them to sit down. She did not smile. She completed signing the documents and she rang the bell. A peon came in and took the folder and went out. She then gazed at the women seated before her, "Which one of you is Mrs. Tharani?"

"I am," said Tharani.

The Principal removed her spectacles, and rubbed it with a piece of soft cloth and put it on. She looked directly at Tharani and said, "I will not mince words, Mrs. Tharani. I will come straight to the point. Both your girls have been expelled."

Tharani's eyes widened in horror, "But. ."

The Principal lifted her hand, "There is nothing you can say that will make me consider otherwise. Your daughter, Sitara, walked into class today with her blouse buttons undone. When the teacher reprimanded her, she undid the last two buttons too.. leaving her blouse completely open. This is a school of repute, and it's a co-ed school. I'm sorry, but there is nothing we can do, no way we can reconsider keeping them."

Tharani pleaded, "Yamini..."

"Yes... Yamini. We are really sorry this has happened and she has to leave too. A brilliant child. In fact, our one chance of a state-level student. That's why this is not a hasty decision. We did a background check..."

She did not elaborate, and indeed, there was no need for her to elaborate. A background check would have revealed the shady family history.

"I would suggest that you take the girls home immediately. You can collect the transfer certificate and other documents later. In such cases, it is generally preferred that we warn other schools about admitting such students, but in this case, I'm not going to do that. In fact, I will write out a recommendation to another school explaining the circumstances and requesting them to admit your daughters. They will do so on the assurance that this kind of behaviour will not be repeated. It's not a prestigious school, but it will do very well. I hope Yamini will be able to take her board exams from there."

The women were silent. Tharani was looking down and tears poured incessantly down her face.

"You may leave now. Thank you."

And the Principal got up and went over to the window and looked out.

Shanthi placed a hand on Tharani's arm. "Come, let's go." She led Tharani out and they walked down the longest corridor of their lives. They were ushered into a room, and they walked in and saw the two girls seated in a corner, looking forlorn, lost, and terrified.

Sitara's eyes were wide with fear as she looked at her mother. Gone was the angry defiant girl of the morning, and in its place was a terrified child. Yamini's face was red with crying and she buried her face once again in her hanky and cried. Shanthi moved forward and said briskly, "You girls pick up your bags. Let's go." No one moved. She then picked up the bags and moved to the door. Tharani looked at her, then back at the girls. She moved forward. "Yamini, let's go."

Sitara tugged at her sari, "Ma!"

Tharani ignored her. "Yamini, come on, let's go!"

The tug increased, "Ma!"

Yamini got up and followed her mother. Tharani turned to Sitara. "Come!" she said. Sitara got up. She ran over to her mother, flung her arms around her and burst into tears. Tharani let her cry. Then she disengaged herself. "We have to leave now."

Sitara nodded and followed her out. No one was out there except the management staff and the office boys. Classes were going on and they could hear the distant voice of a teacher talking, explaining. The girls felt extremely humiliated and walked blindly out, only wanting to get away from it all. They felt eyes boring down their backs, passing judgements. The cab was waiting out for them, and they climbed in.

Once back home, Tharani went into her bedroom and locked herself in. Yamini moved to the other bedroom and closed the door too. Shanthi placed the bags on the table. Sitara moved to the far corner and curled up on the sofa. She looked around. There was a sheet hanging outside, in the porch. She got up and pulled it down and covered herself with it and curled up again. Shanthi watched her, "You might as well take off your clothes now and get comfortable." A sarcastic comment that came to her lips was not voiced because she knew that they, the adults, were the actual perpetrators, not this child who had lost her innocence out of no fault of her own. She held her peace and went to the kitchen. She made tea, poured it into two cups, placed the cups on a tray and a plate of biscuits and came back to the hall. She shook Sitara and said, "Get up. You must eat something."

"I don't want anything."

"You must eat. Get up."

The authoritative voice worked and Sitara got up. Shanthi handed her two biscuits and a cup of tea. She then took two biscuits and a cup of tea and sat comfortably in a chair opposite the girl. They were silent for a while, concentrating on eating.

"Sitara... sorry this happened."

Sitara looked at her, "Why are you sorry? What did you do?"

"I... we immigrants are all the same. It doesn't matter if your mother apologizes or I do. It's all the same."

Sitara sipped her tea, "If this is life, I don't want it," she said.

Shanthi looked at her sharply, "This is life. You are alive because we never thought along those lines...ever. Not when our houses were bombed, taking with it everything we had and the life that we knew. Not when we walked across the Himalayas; not even when our kith and kin died in front of our eyes. We always thought we'd survive, we'd live, we'd make it work. It's that spirit that has kept us going, kept us alive."

"At what expense?" asked the child, sadly.

Shanthi sipped her tea thoughtfully, "Maybe that wasn't necessary. Maybe that was greed. Maybe your mother has fallen so low that she did not know where to draw the line. And maybe it's up to you to draw the line and place boundaries."

Sitara listened carefully.

"Your father might not be coming back."

Sitara looked sharply at her, "Why?"

"He's with another woman now."

"What! I'll kill him!"

"Sure," said Shanthi, "take a train to Bombay and kill him."

Sitara was quiet, "He's not divorced. He's still my mother's husband. Bastard! Pimp!"

She spat.

Shanthi finished her tea and biscuit. She got up and took the cup from Sitara and placed both cups on the tray. "Maybe it wasn't such a bad thing that happened at school. Maybe you would have had to drop out anyways."

"What about the money that we got from... you know. From Ramesh?"

"I think your mother sent it all to your father in the faith that he will invest in the business, and I think it has now disappeared into the woman's pocket."

Sitara's eyes filled with tears. She did not notice that her mother had come out of the room and had heard the conversation. "He sold my virginity to a prostitute?"

"She's not exactly a prostitute."

"She's living with another woman's husband. She's worse than a prostitute. And yes, I am aware that my own mother stoops to the same dirty levels. I don't want this life!"

Shanthi turned and saw Tharani standing there transfixed and staring. She took the tray and moved past her to the kitchen, where she stayed, washing up.

Tharani did not move. "Ma!" said Sitara, but Tharani did not answer. All that she could think of was that her world had come crashing down, and the debris lay at her feet. Her husband was gone; the hard-earned money—even if it was dirty money—was gone; and her children had been expelled from school. She had nowhere to go, no money, and she had three girls to look after.

"Ma!" Sitara came over to her mother and shook her, "Ma! Wake up!"

Tharani moved like a zombie to a chair and sat down, looking glassily ahead, staring at nothing.

The other bedroom door opened and Yamini came out. She came over to Sitara and said, "I want to talk to you." She took Sitara by the hand and led her to the bedroom and closed the door. "Sit down," she said to Sitara. Sitara sat down at the edge of the bed. Yamini stood over her and looked down. There was sadness and love in her eyes, "I'm sorry, Sitara." She sat down on the floor and took her little sister's hands, "I'm sorry I did not protect you. Forgive me."

Sitara looked at her sister's gentle face looking up at her and her lips trembled, "I'm sorry too, Yamini. I was so selfish, thinking only about myself. I forgot that you...that you...I was thinking... oh! I wasn't thinking! I'm so sorry I did this to you!!" She burst into tears. The two girls hugged each other and cried their hearts out.

Eventually, they disengaged and Yamini said, "Sitara, I promise you—and this is a promise for life. I will never ever allow anything to happen to you any more or to Sheila. That is a promise."

Sitara shook her head, "That's not the promise I want. Promise that we—none of us—not you, not mom, not Sheila, and not me—will ever do anything like this again. We will never ever sell our bodies for money. Promise me that."

Yamini placed a hand on her Sitara's head, "I promise. We promise."

The girls felt a sudden strength in their resolve. They felt strength in knowing that the wrong window had been closed shut once and for all, and that they will surely find the right path soon.

"Did you hear about Daddy?"

Yamini nodded, "I did. We must wait for things to come to a head. They will. Meantime, I have to look out for a job."

"Me too."

"And Sheila must continue to go to school."

"Yes."

Out in the hall, Shanthi had taken leave. She had not bid Tharani goodbye as Tharani continued to stare into space. She had pressed her shoulder, "I'll come back later. We'll work out something." When there was no answer, she said urgently, "Don't do anything foolish. Keep the girls in mind."

She then left. Half-an-hour later, there was a knock on the door. Tharani did not bother to open it. Yamini and Sitara came out of the room, and Yamini crossed over and opened the door. It was Ramesh. "Can I come in?" he asked.

Yamini hesitated, "It's not the best of times," she said.

"Please."

She opened the door wide and he came in. He took his seat opposite Tharani and took her hands, "I heard," he said.

She looked at him, "You heard that the girls were expelled. Did you hear that my husband is now with another woman?"

"What! No, I didn't hear that. I'm sorry. It's all come at the same time, hasn't it?"

Tharani did not answer. "Listen, you, Tharani and the girls, I want to talk to you."

"But we want to talk to you first," said Yamini, "There is something I... we wish to tell you."

Tharani looked up at her daughters, startled, "Yes?" asked Ramesh.

"We... my mother, Sitara, Sheila, and I... will never go down the wrong path again. We will never do anything that is hurtful and wrong. We will never sell our bodies for money again."

Tharani and Ramesh listened to them. Tharani's eyes were wide with surprise. Not sell their bodies? How were they going to survive? But Ramesh smiled, "Yes, I think that's a wise decision. I'm sorry I was the way I was. I don't want to be like that anymore either."

They looked startled. "You don't?" asked Sitara, incredulously.

"No. Look, I know it's a bit late to ask, but I would like to think of you girls as my sisters... my family."

Despite her better judgement, Sitara snorted, "Good God! He's reborn! So now it's all incest."

Ramesh glared at her, "I'm surprised they took so long to throw you out."

"At least I grew up faster than you did, possibly because I'm not a zamindar kid. Boy! You people take your time growing!"

Ramesh laughed and Yamini smiled. And somehow everything was alright between the girls and him, possibly because they were all so young.

"I came with some good news," Ramesh continued, "my sister studied in the *** convent. My family... my father is one of the trustees. I have spoken to the Principal. I... I told her the truth. I told her it was bad judgement on your part, Sitara, and that I was giving her my word that it would never happen again. So, if all of you will come with me now, we can wrap up the admissions and you girls can continue with your education where you left off...from next week on—and in a better school."

They stared at him incredulously. He turned to Tharani, and he took her hands, "I also have other news... . I'm getting married. I'm getting married this coming Saturday. My father, he knows all about... .us. He spoke at length to me and he feels it's time I settled down and took over the responsibilities of running the estate."

"What!!" said Sitara, the outspoken one, "A girl is actually willing to marry you? She must be bonkers."

Ramesh looked hurt, "That's true. I'm past redemption apparently."

"Who's this girl?"

"I don't know. Some headmaster's daughter," Ramesh said, uncertainly, "Daddy said she was the only girl willing to marry me because she has a dosha in her horoscope and that she is squint-eyed and one leg is slightly shorter than the other."

"Squint-eyed and limping? You're okay with that?"

He shrugged, "I'm worse off than her, am I not? I don't deserve her...or anybody."

They were silent.

"Anyway, this might be my last visit...at least in a while. I...my wife and I are leaving for Malaysia after the wedding. We have an estate there and my father feels I should get away and take care of it for a while. For a couple of years, in fact. So I want to ask you something," he turned to Tharani, "I want to fund the girls' education completely. I want to see them through college, all three of them. Please allow me to do that."

Tharani stared at him as did the girls, "But...but why would you want to do that?" she asked.

"Because you're family. Because I like your spirit, the way you fight out your way in the world. You came here with almost nothing, but you fought to hold. And now, they are my sisters. I want to see them happy. I have the resources to help them, and I want to do it. Please don't say no."

Tharani looked at the girls with tears in her eyes. She could not speak. The girls were crying too.

Yamini put out her hand, "Ramesh, you don't know how much we are indebted to you. Our own father has betrayed us...but you... Thank you! On behalf of my mother and sisters, and myself, thank you so much!"

He took her proffered hand, "I understand. But it will be easier, now that I'm taking away the burden of education. For the rest..."

"For the rest, I have my sewing machine," said Tharani. They all looked at her. She actually smiled. "Relax, all of you! I'm good with my needle."

They smiled too, "Yey!" said Sitara.

"We must move," said Yamini, "We must move to a different locality."

"Yes," agreed, Ramesh. "I'll give you the money for rent for the first couple of months."

Yamini looked embarrassed, so he added, "Look, I'm quite sure you're going to earn well. You're too smart and intelligent. It's only a matter of time. You can repay me then. I promise I'll take it back with interest."

She smiled then. "Okay then, come on, let's go to this school and sort out the admissions."

It turned out to be a beautiful day after all. The girls were admitted in the school, and it was as prestigious a school as the one they had been in. Ramesh took them out shopping after that and they got the material for the school uniforms, which, of course, would be stitched by their mother. They bought other necessities, and then, they lunched out.

"Let's go to the temple," said Sitara. "We all have solemn vows to take. To never go down the wrong path again. You too, Ramesh."

He nodded. So they went to the temple. Soon, it was time to say goodbye. "Well," Ramesh, "This is it." He looked at Tharani, and then at the two girls. "Take care. I'll always know your whereabouts. I'll always find out. And I will keep sending you money."

"Thank you," said Yamini, on behalf of all of them, "Have a wonderful married life. And wish you all the very best."

Ramesh turned to Sitara, "Be good."

She smiled, "I will." But her lips trembled and she turned and ran into the temple.

Ramesh turned to Tharani and a look of understanding passed between them. He nodded to her, then turned and left without looking back.

Despite so many setbacks, it was a fairly happy set of women who went to sleep that night. But the next day held a different kind of nightmare...

The older girls had no school the next day, but Sheila did. So while Yamini and Sitara slept, Tharani got up to get the little girl ready and off to school. Her bus came in at 8 am. Hardly had she seen the girl off and settled down with a cup of coffee than the doorbell rang. Tharani got up and opened the door. Sushanth stood at the doorway. Tharani looked at him with hatred, hardly wanting to let him in.

"May I come in?" he asked, and she moved aside to let him in. He was carrying a small suitcase, and he placed this on the sofa. He then sat down and removed his shoes. He looked up at Tharani, standing and staring belligerently at him. "How are you?" he asked. "Still alive," she replied, her face wooden and devoid of any expression. "What brings you here?"

"Please Tharani!" he reached out for her, but she moved back instantly, "No! Don't you dare touch me!"

He put down his hand, defeated.

"How long have you been living with that whore?"

"She's not a whore!"

"Really?"

"Look... I... I'm sorry..."

"About what? You gave her all the money, all the jewels I sent you?"

He did not say anything. "Do you realize what your girls and I have been through to feed your girlfriend?"

"Yes, I know. I know I've been a bad father and husband. I'll repay, I promise."

"With what?"

"I'll send you and the girls money every month. Please Tharani!"

"But you're going to continue to live with her?"

"Yes. Actually, that's why I came here. I... I want you to sign the divorce papers..."

Tharani left the room. She came back with a broom and started to hit him with it, right and left, right and left. His screams woke up the girls and they came running out.

"Mamma! What's going on? Oh, Daddy!"

Tharani stopped beating him when she saw the girls. They stared at their father, and he stared back at them. And then, Sitara said words that no father should ever have to hear, "Why did you stop? Hit him harder."

Tharani raised the broom, but Yamini intervened and took the broom away from her and threw it away. "No Mamma! No. He is our father."

Yamini turned to her father and said quietly, "Why are you here?"

"I want a divorce…"

"Oh, okay." She turned to her mother, "It's your decision. You can hand it to him and get it over with or refuse and punish him for being unfaithful. He will never be able to marry her that way."

"Ooooo!!" said Sitara, "I like that!"

"Keep quiet, Sitara!" said Yamini, "Mom, I would advise you to give him the divorce and let him go. It will be closure for you."

Tharani nodded, "Yes, I don't want to remain married to this dog!" She spat at him.

Sushanth slunk over to his suitcase and took out the papers. She signed them and threw them back at him. "Now get out of the house!" she said.

He picked up the papers, put them in his suitcase, and walked out.

He did not see the panic building up in his girls' hearts. Sitara moved restlessly from one foot to the other, her eyes brimming with tears, and Yamini stood there crying, the tears flowing down her face. "Daddy!" said Sitara, and he turned. She ran to him and flung herself in his arms. "Don't go! Don't leave us and go!"

He held her close. She was crying loudly now. Tharani went into the bedroom and shut the door. Yamini looked uncertainly at the closed bedroom door. Should she go after her mother? She turned back to look at her father. Their eyes met over Sitara's head buried in his chest. Yamini came over.

"Do you have to go?"

He nodded shamefacedly, "Yes."

Sitara's tears stopped and she became still. She extricated herself from his arms.

"What do you mean you have to go? You're leaving your family, your wife and your children, and you have to go?"

"I…"

"You what? You love that lady? Is that what you're saying?"

Yamini laid a warning hand on Sitara's shoulder, "Sitara!"

And suddenly, the man standing there was no longer their father. He was a stranger. A dirty, unprincipled, unscrupulous stranger.

"Get out!"

"Sitara, don't!" pleaded Yamini, although she was sick to her stomach.

But Sitara removed her hand from her shoulder. "You leave right now! Go back to your whore. And don't you dare show your face again!"

She looked around for something to throw at him, but Yamini blocked her and turned to Sushanth, "Please leave!"

He turned, opened the door, and walked out.

they said the moon was waning, it would be gone all too soon
but the sky flooded with soothing light – 'twas the Full Moon!

"So what's all this? Who're you getting married to?" asked Ramesh's friend, Vivek.

They were all there on the terrace, Ramesh's friends, on the eve of his wedding, at his bachelorette party, if it could be called that.

No fanfare at this wedding. Just some close relatives had been informed, and Ramesh had invited his friends over. They were to stay with him overnight and till the wedding was over the next day. They were young men who had grown up together. It was night, and the moon was out. It would be full moon tomorrow, on the wedding day. Stars shone in the sky, bright and big. The cool night air blew around.

Ramesh poured out a drink for Vivek and handed it to him, "I don't know," he said.

"What do you mean you don't know? You don't know who you're marrying?"

"No," said Ramesh, half-sitting on the railing, and sipping his drink. "She's the daughter of the headmaster of the village school. Lives in a very remote village... a very village girl."

"And why did you agree to this?"

Ramesh was silent. He looked up at the night sky, the almost full moon. "It's time I settled down."

"So... settle down. Why do you have to get married?"

"Because my father wants me to."

He turned back to his friends, "I've been in a relationship with somebody... you must have heard."

"Right! We heard that!" Rashid said from his perch on the floor. He opened his mouth to tease, but Vivek flashed him a warning look.

"People say they are not good.... People who don't know them. You know..."

They nodded understandingly, but not really understanding. Rashid looked confusedly at Vivek. So he voiced it for them, "How can they be good? How can a family that enamours a young man and takes all his money be good?"

"The parents maybe, yes, but there are the children. Three girls."

"You... ??"

Ramesh shrugged, "I think of them as my family. I love them."

"So do you intend going back to them after your marriage?"

"No. That's over. And I won't be doing anything stupid anymore. But the point is, I haven't been a good person. I've... I've robbed from my mother... jewels... money. I've gone astray."

"And so, you let your father talk you into this marriage to a strange girl."

"I trust my parents."

"Right!" said Rashid, unable to contain himself any longer, "It's dawned on you finally, I suppose."

Ramesh turned to him, "Yes, it has. It's late but at least it's dawned."

They laughed. "How's the girl? Any idea?"

Ramesh stared intently at the glass, "I'm told that she is well educated and ran the school with her father. Her father died recently. I'm also told that she squints... and that she limps. One leg is slightly shorter than the other."

"What??!!"

His friends stared at him incredulously. "And you said yes because... ?" asked Anil.

Ramesh turned to him, "Look, I'm not perfect okay? If you could see my soul, it's black and perforated. Squint eyes and limp weds perforated black soul. We're the perfect couple. Well matched. Who am I to choose or complain?"

"But…" said Vivek.

But Ramesh held up his hand, "This is my wife you're talking about, and I'd rather you did not say anything more. Please!"

Vivek sighed. "Okay. But I need a strong drink."

They all laughed and went back to partying.

The day of the wedding dawned bright and sunny with a blue blue sky and lovely white clouds. Despite the temperance, there was the unmistakable air of festivities in the air. Everyone looked happy. It seemed that the animals felt it too. The horses neighed, the dogs wagged their tails, the cat sat on the wall, preening and cleaning itself and basking in the sunlight.

A servant was sent to wake up the boys early morning, and they got up reluctantly. The servant was an old man who had been with the family before the children were born and he was treated more like a family member than a servant. Ramesh and Meenakshi called him "Babuji Uncle" and neither of them knew why they called him that.

"Babuji, please pulled down the curtains! It's too bright!" Ramesh complained.

"Get up baba. The girl's people will be here soon. You're getting married today. You can't afford to sleep. Wake up."

He soon had the disgruntled boys out of bed. They bathed and came down to breakfast. In the big, wide hall, the swing had been tied up out of the way and the mandap had been set with the brick stones in a square at the centre for the wedding. A fire would be lit there. Ramesh donned the white dhoti and he sat down on one side, leaving a place vacant next to him for his bride to sit. The priest began the ceremony. Soon Devika was brought in, and she walked ever so gracefully and sat down next to Ramesh. And that's when all of Ramesh's friends had apoplexy. They gestured to him wildly and pointed to the girl. He did not turn in her direction but instead he watched his friends, puzzled and confused. "What?" he asked, and they gestured again wildly, pointing to Devika. Rudra and Savitri and Meenakshi were grinning from ear to ear. Then, Meenakshi bent and whispered in her brother's ears, "I think they want you to look at the girl."

And Ramesh turned and looked at her. She turned to him and gave him the sweetest smile. He gaped at her, open-mouthed. And before he could stop himself, he exclaimed, "You don't squint! You're beautiful!"

The smile disappeared and she glared indignantly at him, "Of course I'm beautiful. And excuse me! I don't squint!"

"Ah! But she limps," said Rudra, who was standing close by and looking blissfully innocent.

Devika glared her father-in-law, "Appa! I don't limp!"

He roared with laughter, so infectious, it set everyone laughing.

The priest looked around disapprovingly. "The auspicious hours are slipping by. Can we get on with the marriage?"

They nodded, but it took a while for everyone to settle down and stop smiling. When Ramesh got up to go around the fire with his bride, he could see that she was indeed extremely beautiful and walked gracefully and without any limp.

"Appa! How could you do this?" he whispered fiercely to his father.

Rudra grinned at him happily, "You should have seen your face. Priceless! So worth it! Payback time!"

Later that night, Ramesh stood at the far end of the terrace, looking up at the stars thoughtfully... His wife, Devika, walked in and up to him with a glass of milk. He turned to her, "Why did you marry me?" he asked her abruptly, "You knew I was not a good person, didn't you? Or did they fool you?"

She placed the glass of milk on the railing, "No... no one fooled me."

"Then why did you...?"

She blushed and looked down at the floor, "Because...I..."

"Because you what?" he asked, sharply.

"Because...you married me long back."

"What??!!"

"I was lost in the fair and you found me, and when you took me home, you put a chain around my neck and said, "Now we're married.""

"I never..." he started to say, then remembered, "Oh! So that was you?"

She nodded.

"But you were a child!"

She nodded again, "Yes. I was 10 years old. But see!" She searched among the numerous chains around her neck, and she took out one— multi-coloured gypsy beads strung together, "I still have it."

Ramesh looked at the chain wonderingly.

"Oh my!" he said, overwhelmed. "This is…" he looked at her innocent face and hesitated, not wanting to tell her how absurd it was. "I don't know what to say! Is that why you married me?"

She nodded happily, "And I saw you. I saw you daily, going by on your bike…with your friends. I was in school, then I went to college. I saw you!"

She was blushing now. Comprehension dawned on Ramesh's face, "Ah! And you fell in love with me!"

"Yes," she said, now quite rosy with embarrassment.

He looked down at her, loving her more and more by the minute.

"You know, I'm so glad to hear this. It's not… Oh! Never mind what it is and is not!"

He put his arms around her, pulled her closed, and kissed her, "I promise you this: I will never ever cheat on you. Ever!"

And the full moon and the bright stars bore witness to his promise.

CHAPTER 11

moon had seen it all, it was time to make amends
spread her gentle moonlight before darkness descends

Sitara was driving. The car right in front of them was moving rather slowly. They could see the driver grinning at them in the rear mirror. "Wretch!" said Sitara, "Wait till I show him!" And she stepped on the gas. The car shot off like a rocket, and as they passed the car in front, Sitara honked and honked. "Wheeee!!" She screamed at the driver, "That will teach you a lesson, you road-hogging rogue." Suddenly the man turned into a cop, and he set the police siren going. "Wheeeeee!!" They were in trouble! "Wheeeee....!!"

Tharani woke up with a start. The alarm was ringing. She had been dreaming. Sigh... Sitara was troublesome even in dreams. Tharani reached out and switched off the alarm. She reached up to her hair and lifted it all up to the top of her head and made a knot. Then she adjusted her night gown and got out of bed. She went over to the bathroom, brushed her teeth and had a shower and changed into a sari. She then put on a bindi. After all, Sushanth wasn't dead. They were just divorced. The bindi was so much a part of Tharani's appearance, it was impossible for her to think of giving it up. She then made her way to the kitchen and filled the kettle with water and set it to boil. She hummed as she made her coffee and took it to the hall to drink it in peace and read the newspaper.

Life had been good these past six years. They had indeed travelled a long, long way. She still remembered those two days so clearly just as if it had all happened recently. The girls being expelled, admitting them in a different school, Ramesh bidding them goodbye.... Sushanth asking for divorce. She had lost contact with Sushanth. Shanthi had moved to Bombay to be with her husband. There were no other means by which to be updated, but since she had not heard from him, she presumed he was okay. Shanthi had written in regularly in the beginning, but with passing years, the communication had petered out. Tharani was not very worried. She had to live her own life. She had to take care of the girls, educate them, and get them married.

They had moved to a different locality almost immediately. The house had been smaller, but Tharani was able to reinstate her tailoring business. When the people there realized that the family was okay and not up to any funny activities, they became quite friendly. The girls had done well in the new school. They had made quite some friends too. Ramesh kept in touch with them through mails. He never called or visited, but he had sent them money regularly till Yamini started working. He was now the proud father of a boy and a girl. Sheila now studied in the same school as the other two girls had, under Ramesh's recommendation.

Yamini had completed college two years back. She had immediately got placed in a multinational company. Sitara was following closely in her footsteps and was in the last year at college. Sitara worked part-time as a receptionist at a hospital in the evenings. Yamini had done part-time jobs too while still at college. This allowed the girls to buy and maintain a car and helped out some with the finances. A year after she started working, Yamini applied for a housing loan and they were able to move into their own modest flat in the same area. So now Tharani had her own house! Her children had all grown up to be fine young women. She could not have asked for more. Well, maybe she could. She dreamt of the day when Yamini would get married. She would then have a baby, and she, Tharani, would be a grandmother. She felt there could no greater joy than that. She would, of course, take care of the baby... that was her favourite daydream.

Yamini had written to Ramesh requesting that she be allowed to repay the money they had taken from him and to please quote an amount. He wrote back an amount that wasn't even close to the amount he had spent on them. In fact, it was an amount that could be repaid in easy instalments in five years. He requested her not to argue, that he considered her his sister, that he had funded them only because he could afford it. She could do nothing but agree, but she decided that when Sitara started working too, she would repay a similar amount each month for a separate five years. Sitara agreed to it because it really was a very affordable amount to repay each month.

Tharani finished her coffee, picked up her cup, and started to make her way back to the kitchen when the doorbell rang. "What the... ! It's only 7 am!" The maid of course! "I told her to come in later." Tharani opened the door, and when she saw who stood there, she froze. It was Sushanth. He looked tired and shabby, his hair was in disarray. And he held on to a suitcase. He stood there, his eyes pleading. "Tharani, please may I come in?"

And she just stood there, her eyes down, her face wooden and devoid of any expression. She did not move.

"Tharani please! Please!"

She moved aside and he walked in. He looked around at the hall. It was not a big hall, but tastefully decorated and homely. He turned to Tharani.

She still stood at the door, her eyes down, her face still expressionless. She was as still as a statue.

"Tharani, I…"

She looked up then with such fierce anger, "Why are you back? What do you want?"

Sushanth placed the suitcase on the floor. And then, he fell flat at her feet, and started crying loudly, "I'm sorry! I'm so sorry! Please forgive me! Please forgive me!"

Tharani looked at his prostate form on the floor and felt nothing but disgust. She moved away from him.

The girls heard the wailing and rushing out of their room. "Mamma! What happened?!! Oh!"

They saw their father there on the floor, his arms outstretched, wailing.

He continued to cry and say, "I'm so sorry! I've been a fool! Please forgive me!"

Sitara looked with horror from him to her mother. Sheila looked on wide-eyed. Yamini looked down with concern at her father.

She moved towards him, and she bent down and touched his head. "Daddy, please get up. You're scaring Sheila. Whatever it is, we can sit and talk. Please get up."

She turned to Sitara, "Sitara, please go make Daddy a cup of coffee."

She turned to Sheila. "Sheila, go and run the water for the bath."

"Wait!" said a voice. Yamini turned.

"I won't stay here if he does," said Tharani firmly, "You decide."

Yamini looked at her mother, "We will talk things out, Amma. He's tired."

"There's nothing to talk. Send him out right now or I leave!"

Sitara looked on interestedly. She gave the cup of coffee to her father. He placed it on the table and looked sadly at Tharani.

Yamini went up to her mother. "You can't talk like that. You know you can't. Please come in and hear what he has to say. We'll decide what to do after that."

Tharani did not answer.

"He is our father. What do you expect us to do?"

There was silence for a while... Then Tharani came in. She went into the next room and stood near the wall, at the back of the door, where she could listen clearly to the conversation without being seen.

Yamini took a chair and sat opposite her father, "Why are you back Daddy?"

He looked at his eldest. "I've lost everything Yamini. I... I've been a fool. I... I trusted her."

"The woman?"

"Yes."

"What's her name?"

"Veera."

"Okay."

"She took all my money, my savings, and she left me and ran away. She and her brother."

"Oh."

"Yes, they left overnight."

"They fled?"

"Yes. We've not been able to track them."

Yamini nodded. "It won't be easy. They must have planned it well, covered their tracks."

"Yes."

"So now you have nothing left and nowhere to go, is that it?"

"Yes. I... I'm so sorry I left you all. I'm so, so sorry!"

"But Daddy, you realize you're divorced from Amma right?"

"Yes."

"So what is it you want us to do? You can't both stay here together. And she stays here. That's final. It's not even a consideration that she leave. So, what is it that you wish us to do?"

His voice was low and choked up, "Please allow me to stay."

Yamini stared at him.

"Where will I go?"

"Appa, you can't stay here, you know that."

"I promise not to trouble her. I won't even go near her. Just give me a small corner in your house to keep my things and sleep. I'll eat out. I won't disturb you all in any way. I promise."

Yamini looked helplessly at him. She wanted to help him but she knew very well that this was not going to work. Her mother...

"Yamini, could you please come in for a moment?" said Tharani.

Yamini got up and nodded to her father. She then went in and behind the door where Tharani stood.

"Yes, Amma?"

"He can stay."

"But..."

"I'll manage. He can stay here in the spare room. I'll cook for him as well, but he is not to be in the same room as I am. He is not to speak to me. Ever."

Yamini listened seriously, then she looked down and was silent, thinking deeply.

"Okay. I'll tell him that for now. But if it doesn't work out, I'll check out if I can get him some alternate accommodation. Also, he must work. It's a must. I'll talk to the hotel owner at the end of the road. They are looking for a cashier."

Tharani nodded.

Yamini went back to the hall. Sushanth, of course, had heard their discussion.

"Well, Appa?"

He nodded. "It's okay by me. I'd only be too glad to be working again."

Yamini smiled at him, "Come, let me take you to your room."

He got up and followed her into the house. Right at the back was a small store room.

"You can stay here," said Yamini. "There's a separate bathroom and restroom at the back. Please use that."

He nodded.

Yamini hesitated, then said, "Daddy?"

"Yes Yamini?"

"Please... Please don't talk to Sitara or Sheila. They're not used to... They've been through a lot. Please wait to see if they accept you."

He nodded. He was crying again. "Yes. I understand. Yamini... ."

"Yes Daddy?"

"Thank you."

Her lips trembled, but she nodded in acknowledgement and left the room.

Tharani's mind was in turmoil. She did not know what to make out of the situation. It could not go on forever surely—living in the same house as her ex-husband and cooking for him. And as was her wont whenever she was in trouble, she had a bath, got dressed, and left for the temple. She did her puja, then settled down under the tree to think. This tree and this temple had been her refuge and her succour. Although there were three children in the house, it had been a lonely journey. There were no adults to talk to, no one to share her worries. Shanthi had left too. Even now, she was alone. She wished she could call out to a friend and talk. But there was no one: just herself and her God. What was there to think? He had returned. He had left that woman and come back. Tharani felt an unreasonable rage against the woman who had stolen her husband—if there was any such thing. Women don't steal. The man has a brain and he doesn't use it very much. But the woman had dared to cheat, she had dared to rob and abscond. Tharani spent several pleasant moments imagining what she would do to that woman if she ever caught her. She wondered if she should do some puja against her? She decided against it. It was never good to do negative pujas more than necessary. Karma was a bitch. Besides, she had promised the children to walk down the straight path, and she meant to keep that promise.

She abandoned her plans and thoughts about 'that woman' (as she called her) and returned back to thinking about Sushanth and what his return to the family meant. Nothing offered itself. He was back and only time will tell if it can be worked out and whether he could really stay all his life with them....not talking to her, not being in the same room as her but living in the same house. Then an alarming thought struck her. She was on the verge of looking out for bridegrooms for Yamini. How would this affect that? What should she do... say. She decided to be honest and tell the truth. Then God willing, it will all work out.

Not for a moment did it occur to Tharani to think that Yamini was her source of income and what could happen to her and her other two girls should Yamini get married. The house was hers too. Where would they all go? Tharani was a lioness. She knew she would survive. She could not live at the cost of her daughter's happiness. Yamini must get married. After all, that is what the struggle had been about all along—to see the children educated and settled. And then, of course, to become a grandmother... Tharani became engrossed, once again, in that daydream. She smiled to herself. Everything will be alright.

Days slipped by...

Sheila had been peeking into her father's room off and on. She was in her early teens now, but she remembered distinctly being carried by him, being bought toys, being flung up in the air, sitting on his big, broad shoulders... She wanted to talk to him but she was too shy. Sushanth noticed her frequently passing by his room, which was odd because his room was right at the end of the house. Sometimes the shadow lurked outside his door. And he moved to the door and looked out and smiled at her. That was her undoing.

"I came first in class."

"Aha? Congratulations!" he said, smiling. "You have your report card?"

"Yes," she moved nervously from one foot to the other.

"May I see it?"

"Yes."

She went to her bedroom and brought it. Sushanth had gone into his room and she hesitated at the door. She looked outside and could not see her mother or sisters. She went in.

When Yamini came home, she paused at her bedroom door. She could hear laughter from her father's room. Sheila and Sushanth... .

She smiled to herself and went into her own bedroom. She had been spending time with her father too, talking to him... man to man now. She was his eldest.

Sitara ignored Sushath's presence completely. When asked to give him his food, she just kept it inside his room and walked out. He tried talking to her but she did not respond. She showed no interest in him whatsoever and pretended he did not exist.

Then, one day, it rained heavily. Sitara had her own two-wheeler. She was driving home when it started to rain. She had to stop and take shelter. But eventually, the rain petered to a drizzle but there was a lot of thunder and lightning. She got on her bike and drove home. Half-way through, she had to pass a highway with fields on either side. As she drove on, she noticed a man standing under a tree by the roadside. She passed him, but something about him was rather familiar. Her dad! What was he doing here? And why was he standing under a tree in this weather? She swore under her breath and turned back.

Yes, it was him, standing there under the tree, soaked wet.

"You can't do anything right, can you?" she shouted. "You do know you shouldn't be standing under a tree in a thunderstorm, right?"

"There's no other place to stand," he shouted back.

"Come on! Let's go home!"

He came to the road.

She tried hard not to smile, but her lips trembled and the smile was out. He grinned back through wet locks covering his eyes, looking rather boyish. He got on behind her and they set off.

"I'm cold!"

"Yeah, right!" she said, "What are you doing down this road?"

"I went to town to get a pair of slippers."

"Did you?"

"No. Too costly. I'll get some from the cobbler. He makes good slippers."

"I'll take you to town tomorrow. You can pay me later."

"Thank you," he said, humbly.

"You really are shameless," she remarked. "Taking money from your daughter."

"I'm sorry."

"We all are," she replied, "anyways, how's your job going?"

"Good. I'm sitting and counting cash all day long. Free food, wi-fi…"

"Aha? Who are you networking with? Your girlfriend?"

"She's gone. I was talking to Vineeth Uncle."

"What's he saying?"

"He's asking me to get back to Bombay."

"As a partner?"

"No, as a worker."

"Don't do it."

"Right now, no, I don't think so. I want a break."

"And later?"

"I don't know. I don't want to go back."

"Then don't."

"Okay."

"hmmm… .you're docile now all of a sudden, aren't you? Get down."

He got down.

"Had your fangs removed."

He looked at her and grinned. She smiled back.

"Wait," she said as he turned to go in, "I have a towel with me. Rub dry, then go in. You know mom wouldn't like you dripping water all over the place."

He took the towel from her and rubbed himself well with it and gave it back to her.

"What! I'm supposed to carry this in, is it?"

They laughed together.

The interlude set things back to normal between father and daughter and soon Sitara was regaling him with stories about her college life.

Meanwhile, Tharani had started actively looking out for a boy for Yamini. She placed her profile in various matrimonial sites and she passed the word around whenever she went to the temple. Soon, she found the family she was looking for. The lady was divorced and she had a son who was a professor. Tharani was excited. A divorced woman would understand her situation. This just might work out. For Tharani, the added joy was that the boy was from an upper caste…and they were not particular about caste! Tharani had little clue what caste she and Sushanth belonged to, which made her respect the caste system a lot and wish to belong, as mentioned earlier. Overall, she felt it was a good proposal. The thing was would Yamini accept to see the boy? She had shown no interest in men after Ramesh had left and neither had Sitara. Both of them concentrated on working hard and making ends meet. They were also very protective of Sheila.

That evening, she decided to ask Yamini. She waited for the girl to relax after coming back from office. She heard the girls giggling and talking and she went into their room. "Yamini, I need to talk to you."

They all looked at her. "You talk to her right here, right now. No secrets," said Sitara.

Yamini looked at her sister and grinned. "It must be about you. What have you done?"

"Me? I splashed water from a puddle on to a man's white dhoti today," she giggled, "Splash!! You should have seen his face!"

The girls giggled. "Did he scream at you?" asked Sheila.

"Yes!! He said some interesting bad words. Something like…" she said something in Tamil.

Tharani looked horrified, "Sitara, you should really stop doing things like that. And don't say those words. They're unladylike."

"So am I," said Sitara, sagely, "I didn't do it on purpose. He was walking too close to the puddle and there was no other way out."

"You could have stopped and asked him to move on," Yamini pointed out.

Sitara shrugged, "I honked. He was moving so sloooowly. Slow motion…" She pretended to float in the air and flopped on the bed.

None of them could help laughing at the mischievous girl.

Tharani caught Yamini's eyes. She nodded and went out of the room with her mother.

But Sitara called out, "Hey! Not fair! I want to know what's going on! I'm coming!"

Sheila added, "I'm coming too!"

"You stay here," said Sitara, "I'll come and tell you."

The girl pouted but stayed put.

Sitara went to Tharani's room too.

Tharani closed the door.

"Yamini, I've seen this boy's profile in the matrimonial site. And it's perfect."

"Pooh! Is that all?" Sitara exclaimed and flopped down on her mother's bed.

"Yes, so now you know, you can leave," said Tharani, "And don't touch that! Or that! Or that!"

"I'm staying. Who knows, the guy might be just who I'm looking for."

"Yes, he just might be the type to tie a stone around his own neck and drown," Tharani could not resist saying sarcastically.

"And we'd live happily ever after at the bottom of the ocean."

Tharani looked at her with horror-stricken fascination for a while, then she turned to Yamini, "Anyways, as I was saying, I've found the perfect family. The mother is divorced and she has a son. He is a professor. They are interested in you."

Yamini looked round-eyed at her mother, "They are? How do they know me?"

"Well, the profile is put up by his mother. So I guess she is the one who is interested in you. I want to ask them to come over this Sunday."

"You mean you and the mother of the boy are interested in each other. You both should get married."

"Shut up Sitara!" Tharani said, looking like she'd like to swat her daughter.

Yamini's eyes widened, "What! Are you crazy?? This Sunday?"

"Yes," said Tharani, puzzled, "Is there a problem?"

"But... I don't even have any intention of getting married. I haven't thought along those lines at all!"

"I'm not asking you to do anything. Just meet the mother and the boy. There's just the two of them. Then we'll see how it goes. This might not be the person, but we'll get an idea how to go about things."

"Ah well," said Sitara, philosophically, "And there's always the possibility that I might like the boy or the boy might like me better."

"Yes, that too," said Tharani sarcastically, "I'll lock her up in her room for sure."

"You wouldn't," said Sitara, shocked.

"Yes, I think you and Sheila can stay away."

"Try and stop me," said Sitara.

Tharani sighed, "The person I want showing some interest isn't showing any, and the one I want out of my room right now is jumping up and down. Yamini, please say yes, for my sake. It's not a big deal. You're just going to meet some people."

Yamini smiled, "Okay Mummy. Only for your sake. And also maybe Sitara here might like him..."

'Oh! Shut up both of you!" said Tharani, exasperated.

But someone was listening at the door. Someone who then stealthily moved away... Someone who then got dressed and left the house in a hurry...

Later that night, Yamini went into her father's room to give him his dinner.

"What's for dinner?" he asked her.

"Rice and sambar and some vegetable. There's apalam too."

"Sit down, child. I want to talk to you."

Yamini looked sharply at him. Then she placed the food on the side table, closed the door, and came back, and sat down on the bed, opposite him.

"I heard your mother and you and Sitara talking. Is it true she is looking out for a bridegroom for you?"

"Yes... They are coming this Sunday."

"Do you want to get married?"

Yamini shook her head uncertainly, "I don't know... I haven't thought about it. If I liked the boy, then maybe.."

"Have you thought about the consequences?"

"The consequences of getting married? No, not really..."

"Where will we go? Where will your sisters go? This house belongs to you."

"But... of course you will all stay here! I don't think I'll ever marry anyone who will not agree to that."

"There is also the question of your horoscope," he said, looking at her strangely. Her mother would have instantly known he was going to lie.

"My horoscope? I didn't even know I had one."

"Well you have." He reached out to the window sill and took a folder. He gave it to her. "This is your horoscope. I got it made from a jyothishi (astrologer) by giving him your time of birth. There is a problem with it. The boy you marry will die within a couple of years."

"What! No ways!" said Yamini. She opened the folder and tried to read the strange parchment paper in it with nothing but strange signs.

"I can't read this."

"The jyothishi did. He is a famous man. He is never wrong."

"Oh okay. So I can't get married I suppose."

"You can, child. There are ways to get rid of the problem, but you must be honest about it to the person you're going to marry. You must tell them it is so. Also... .you must tell them that you're not a virgin."

Yamini blushed deeply, looked down, and kept quiet. Her lips trembled.

"There's nothing to be ashamed of. Virginity is not a big issue nowadays, but hiding it is an issue. You can't start a relationship with deceit."

Yamini got up and ran out of the room.

Someone had been listening to the whole conversation. Tharani had just been passing by the room when she heard voices and stopped to listen. She now barged into the room and caught Sushanth by his shirt and shook him, "You wretch! You dirty, selfish ***!! How dare you! How dare you talk to her like that!! How dare you come in here and spoil our lives!" And she beat him with her fists, every which way she could. He tried to fend her off but she was furious!

Sitara marched in, looking as furious as her mother, "Oh yes! Beat him up! You made Yamini cry? How dare you?"

"Stop it! Please!" Yamini ran in and fended her mother off.

She pushed her right to the door. "Stop hitting him!"

"Devil!" screamed Tharani, "All he thinks about is himself! His needs, his comfort! Throw him out!"

Yamini took her firmly by the arm and led her out of the room and into her own room and shut the door. "Chill Amma. I'm not a child. I can make my own decisions. I know he's making up the horoscope. But... yes, he's right. They have to know I'm not a virgin."

"But…"

"No buts, said Yamini, firmly, "They have to know. And I... I don't want anyone to know. If you're thinking about what is good for me, you will spare me the pain and call this off. Please!"

She folded her hands and beseeched.

Tharani looked at her. She sighed. "Okay. I'll let this pass for now."

"Thank you."

"Will you throw him out?"

"Where will he go?"

"He can go to hell for all I care!"

"You care, Amma! You care deeply. That's why you let him in. He's your first and last love."

Tharani did not say anything.

"There's nothing he can say or do that will hurt us. We're all mature adults here. He can keep trying."

Tharani got up. "I'm going to my room. I've not known any peace in a while now," she stopped, and then she said, "I think I'll be going out tomorrow morning. Will you manage?"

"Are you going out to the mountains to see the Forest Spirit to put a spell on him? Last time you put a spell, someone died you know."

"No. I won't put any spell on him...not because I don't want to. But I promised you. I'm going because I need to know peace. My mind is a constant state of turmoil."

Yamini nodded understandingly, "Okay you go, but no hanky panky. Promise."

Tharani came up to her, placed a hand on her head and said, "I promise."

Yamini smiled. She knew then that her mother meant it. She would never dream of putting her child's life at stake.

The next day, Tharani woke up early morning. Just like the previous time she had been to see the Forest Spirit, she prepared a complete meal and carefully packed it all in banana leaves and newspapers. She then had a bath and donned a yellow sari with a green blouse. She had to go barefoot, of course. That was a requisite too.

Soon she was in the train and speeding towards the lonesome station. Having been there once, she was more prepared now and less scared. She now trusted the Forest Spirit and felt a bond with her. She got down at the station and watched as the train sped off. Once again, the station of empty of people except for the limping lady station master. The lady looked at her curiously and came limping towards her.

"Haven't you been here before?"

"Yes... I came here a few years back."

"Okay." The lady was curious but she knew she was not supposed to ask the purpose.

Tharani did not enlighten her either. She just picked up the bag and walked out of the station and right up the hill. She found the clearing she had sat in earlier and she took a stick and drew a circle and went within the circle and placed the food outside of it and sat down to wait. She knew it could be a long time. Just sitting there was peaceful. Everything seemed far away... even her troubles. What if she was dead? This is how it would be. The girls would have to deal with their father all by themselves and they would have to survive on their own. She thought about it for a while and came to the conclusion that they would be okay. They were tough girls and had seen and been through a lot. They were resilient. Yamini... she was the finest girl in the world. She was mature, dignified, and trustworthy. A girl in a million. Sitara... Tharani smiled. So like her. So much so that they understood each other like no one else did. She would eventually grow up, but it was doubtful she would ever get over her temper. And little Sheila was growing up so fast! She was beautiful now. So obviously the youngest...much petted and protected. The older ones would always look out for her. They would see that she lived life the way it had been denied them. Tharani was sure of that.

And Sushanth... Tharani felt a pain in her chest. She looked around, and all of a sudden, she felt lonely the way she had never felt before. The only man she had loved had betrayed her in a way they could never get back together, ever. It was goodbye not just in this birth but in all the births to come. No man to love... nobody... "I don't want to be born again," she said aloud. "This should be my last birth. I know I haven't been a good person, but I have learnt all there is to learn."

The leaves fluttered in a sudden gush of wind. A squirrel hopped off the tree and stood on its hind legs and stared at her. Then startled by something it took off. Tharani saw a bright blue light pass swiftly from tree to tree. It grew brighter as it approached her. It was now very bright and on top of a big tree. As Tharani adjusted her gaze, she could make out it was the form of a woman. The Forest Spirit was here. She jumped lightly to the ground and came towards Tharani. Tharani folded her hands and bent to the ground in homage. The Spirit stood there looking down at her. She was the same as before, with a skirt made of leaves covering the lower part of her body, a chain of flowers around her neck. She had a crown of flowers wound around her forehead and flower bangles on her wrists and feet. She was luminescent and powerful...and so beautiful and full of grace! She stepped lightly over the line and placed her hand on Tharani's head. And as if hit by lightning, she removed her hand, and her eyes widened. Tharani looked up and saw a look of shock on her face. "It's my thoughts, isn't it?' she asked. "It's my loneliness that you felt. Please cure me!"

The Spirit looked deeply into her eyes and there was immense love in her own. She calmed down, went into a meditative state and once again placed her hands on Tharani's head. A whirlwind of dry leaves seemed to rush through Tharani's mind. Dry leaves, twigs... pain, they rushed in circles as in a hurricane. They slowly turned to colours. Yellows gave way to blues and reds, which turned to pink... lighter pinks and blues... and greens... light greens... .light pink... .white. The white was serene... peaceful... .eternal. It was soft, comforting, protective, and full of love. Tharani felt peace descend on her. She felt loved the way she had never been loved before. It was unconditional. It was a promise never to let go. And Tharani felt cocooned in that love. And she knew she had arrived home.

She felt a movement on her head and she knew then that the Spirit had withdrawn her hand. But she was in a state of stupor; she still felt this amazing sense of well-being. It stayed with her and she did not open her eyes. Time passed... .time became meaningless.

When she finally opened her eyes, she was alone. Dark shadows everywhere! The birds were flying home. It was evening! She looked around, enjoying the peace. She watched the birds as they noisily tried to settle down for the night. She looked in the distance at the hills on the other side. How high they were! She looked down at the station. She must go home.

It was quite late when she reached home and knocked on the door. The girls and Sushanth had had their dinner. Sheila had fallen asleep. The other two were awake and waiting, worried for Tharani. They knew that she knew her way around, but they still worried. She wasn't all that young anymore...

Yamini ran up and opened the door and Tharani came in. Yamini looked at her mother's face, "You look radiant!" she smiled.

Tharani smiled back, "I feel so happy!"

"What's that?" she asked.

Before Tharani could answer, Sitara walked in, "Where have you been? And why are you smiling so unnaturally?"

Tharani looked at her, "I went to see the Forest Spirit."

"Oh! You know what happened last time, right? You came back with spells... Who are you killing this time?" she asked conversationally.

Tharani frowned, "No one. I went because I needed peace of mind."

"You could have asked me. I would have given you a piece of my mind. Always happy to oblige."

Tharani pretended to shudder, "Go and bring me some water to drink."

"What's in those packages?"

"I bought some gifts for you girls."

"Oh wow!" said Yamini, taking the box that Tharani gave her. She opened it. It contained a pair of shoes that she had been wanting for quite a while.

Tharani gave a package to Sitara. She tore opened the wrapper "Oh wow!" she said. There was a beautiful bag in there.

"You really are very happy!" She stared at her mother.

Tharani smiled back, "I also bought something for Sheila... and Sushanth."

Both girls stared at her now, then Yamini asked incredulously, "You bought something for Daddy?"

"Yes... I just felt he needed some shirts and pants," Tharani was actually shy.

"You're not considering getting back with him, are you?" Sitara asked in her forthright way.

"No! Of course not silly! I just felt like doing something good to let go of all the resentment."

"Hmmm..." said Sitara thoughtfully, "So much blithe happiness is not good for health. But it is good while it lasts. Will you give me something else that I want very much if I ask you now?"

The smile vanished from Tharani's face, "No," she said firmly.

Sitara picked up the bag and the wrapper and turned to leave, "Stupid and useless Forest Spirit!"

Yamini picked up the packet containing the shirt and pant for Sushanth. She knocked on his door. "Come in!" he said.

"Mummy has bought you something," she smiled. He looked at her, not comprehending. She handed him the package. He took it from her and tore it open.

"A shirt and pant! Just what I need!" he said. "Please thank her for me."

"Yes, Appa."

She turned to go. He caught hold of her hand, "Yamini, I'm sorry. I'm really, really sorry!"

She looked down seriously at him, "You've made some very bad mistakes in life, haven't you? That horoscope wasn't mine."

"No... no, it wasn't. I was just scared..."

"Of what? You should know I would never leave you and go!"

"Yes. I should have known that. But after dealing with..."

"Don't compare me to someone so low. Please!"

"Yes. Sorry, I won't."

She relaxed. "Please relax and be alright Appa. I'm not going anywhere."

He looked up at her, and she saw a strange light in his eyes, of unshed tears, "I'm your child now, aren't I? You're the boss. You're my mother."

She smiled, "I remember your lessons. I remember how you carried me on your shoulders when I couldn't walk. I will always be your daughter."

"Then I must behave like a father," he said more to himself.

"I should be going," she said, gently.

He nodded.

That night, around midnight, Tharani heard a soft tap tap sound on her bedroom door. Someone was knocking. She got up in a hurry. The girls! Were they okay?

"Tharani!"

It was Sushanth. "Please open the door!"

Was he kidding her? Why would she open the door? She had made a mistake buying him gifts, hadn't she?

"Tharani!"

She kept quiet, feeling it was not necessary for her to answer. He sounded okay and healthy, so there was nothing going on there that could not wait till morning.

"Do I want to get back with him?" she wondered, "No, of course not! I can never sleep with a man who cheated on me. It's over."

She turned to the other side, but the knocking went on.

"Go away!" she said.

Silence... Then, "Okay, I will. But please say you forgive me. Please! That's all I need to hear."

Tharani relaxed. So that was all it was. He was in one of his remorseful moods. He'd forget all about it and do crazy things again, but he was remorseful tonight. Must have boozed...

"Yes, I forgive you. Now please go back to sleep."

"Do you mean that?"

"Yes, I do."

"Thank you so much Tharani. I will always love you."

She almost snorted but kept quiet. She heard the sound of receding footsteps.

She turned towards the window. The soft moonlight fell on her face. Her sense of well-being continued. Yellow turned to colours... and colours turned to white. It was all white and peaceful. She fell asleep with a smile on her face.

She did not see the gathering dark clouds. She did not see the moon hurry to hide behind them.

The next day was Saturday. The girls didn't have to go to work or college and they rarely woke up early. Tharani woke up, as usual, at 6 and had a bath, donned a sari, combed her hair and powdered her face and placed the bindi between her brows. Then she was all set to relax a bit and have coffee. She made a flask of coffee for Sushanth and placed it on the table. She placed the newspaper next to it. He was an early riser too and would be up any minute now and wanting to read the paper and drink coffee. She switched on the TV and kept it low so as not to disturb the girls. She watched the news and drank her coffee.

Soon she was done. Sushanth was not up yet. She took her cup and saucer and moved to the kitchen and started cooking. She decided she'd make chicken biryani for lunch since the whole family was at home that day.

At half-past 7, Yamini came into the kitchen. "Good morning!" she said brightly, smiling at her mother.

"You're up early!"

"Hmmm... I might go back to sleep. Where's Daddy gone early morning?"

Tharani looked at her, "I don't know. I didn't hear him go out."

"He hasn't drunk his coffee. It's still there."

Tharani's eyes widened. So did Yamini's.

They ran out of the kitchen and to Sushanth's door. It was locked from inside. They banged and banged on it.

"Daddy! Open the door! Daddy!"

"Sushanth! Open the door."

But there was no answer from inside.

Yamini moved back and ran towards the door, but it would not give way.

Then Tharani went to the kitchen and brought a hammer. She hit at where she knew the latch would be. Bang! Bang! Bang!

The latch gave way and the door opened. Meanwhile, Sitara had woken up too, wondering what the noise was all about. So had Sheila.

They opened the door and went in. Sushanth lay there on the bed, his hands hanging loosely on either side. A bottle lay on the floor near his right hand. Tharani went close. His eyes were shut and there was frothing at the mouth.

Her lips trembled. Yamini checked the pulse. She felt his forehead. It was cold. She turned to Sheila. "Sheila, go call Doctor Uncle and ask him to come immediately."

Sheila nodded and ran out. Doctor Uncle was one of their neighbours. The doctor followed Sheila in and went to the bedroom. He went over to where Sushanth lay. He felt his forehead, then lifted and checked for pulse at the wrist. He then went close to the chest and listened. He then used his stethoscope.

"When did you find him like this?"

"Just a few moments ago."

"When did he last talk to any of you?"

"Last night, when I gave him his dinner," Yamini said.

"Past midnight," said Tharani, "He spoke to me then."

The doctor and the girls looked at her. The girls were startled and wide-eyed. This was news to them.

"What did he say?" asked the doctor.

Tharani looked uncomfortable, "He...he asked me to forgive him...said he will always love me."

"Ah, I see!"

The girls and Tharani waited with bated breath.

He turned to Tharani, "Ma'am, I'm sorry to inform you that your husband is dead."

Tharani sank to the floor. The girls watched her, wondering what to say or do.

"It looks like suicide. I need to inform the police. There will be a post-mortem...it will be best for you all to get dressed and ready..."

A sudden wail interrupted him. Tharani was wailing. Yamini sank to the floor next to her mother. Sitara had tears in her eyes. Sheila was crying too. Sitara went over to her and put her arms around her.

Yamini hugged her mother close and she was crying too. The doctor called the police on his cell phone. "Hello," said a voice. He walked out of the room to take the call.

through thunder and lightning
through Sunshine and rain
through all that's frightening
the Moon does still reign...

The days following Sushanth's death were difficult ones, especially because it was a suicide. Queries, police station visits, some more queries, reports to be filed... it went on and on...

Between working and coping with this onslaught, the women had little time to assess how they felt. Dinner table talk helped a lot. It was the only time of the day that they spent together. Tharani had made that a rule.

"Pass me the chapattis," said Sheila.

"Sitara, please serve everyone," said Tharani, sitting down comfortably.

Sitara served them all and sat down. They ate in silence for a while.

"When will it all be over? I'm fed up!" she said.

"Me too!" said Sheila. "Papers, papers, and more papers! Ah bah!"

"It's not just that. I don't know what to think about Daddy's death," said Sitara.

"You have to feel sad," Yamini pointed out.

"I cry a lot," said Sheila, "I cry in my bed. I cry all over my pillow."

"That's good," said Tharani, "You should cry. He was your father. He wasn't all good... as a husband, mostly. But he was a good father. We had some good times."

"I will always remember him for the sacrifices he made to take care of us, especially when we came to Madras. He took care of us all the way. He carried you Sheila. And you too, Sitara," Yamini said.

"Yes, yes, he did!" said Sheila, her voice trembling. "We're so much a family despite everything. We are one unit. I think that's what hurts the most. One of us is gone!"

Tharani nodded, and there were tears in her eyes, "Yes, that's the hardest part. He left me... but he was always a part of me. We understood each other."

"I feel..." said Sheila, hesitantly, "I feel that we could have stopped him... I feel guilty."

They grew silent, each lost in her own thoughts.

"I'm not sure we could have," said Tharani, firmly, "Our reactions were normal. He did and said wrong things and we reacted to it as normal right-thinking people would. He should not have said nor done those things. And he should have had the courage to rectify his mistakes and live. It wasn't all that difficult a thing to do considering he had a roof over his head, a job, food to eat, and people who forgave him easily and loved him. He had a lot going for him and he knew it. He was an immigrant who had seen and dealt with worse situations, and he would surely have known this was not the way out."

Yamini nodded, "Yes, he was rich both in love and money. This was not a right decision. I think it was guilt—guilt that he had failed as father and husband. I think he felt he was a burden now, not a contributing member."

"And I guess he felt that his dying would reduce that and maybe set things right in some way. I think he thought he was doing us a favour," said Sitara.

"He wasn't!" said Sheila, now wailing loudly, "I wish he hadn't died. Oh, Mamma!" and she turned to her mother and put her arms around her and buried her face in her shoulder and cried.

Sitara and Yamini were crying too. No one left the table. "I wish that too!" said Sitara.

They understood each other's sorrow. No one wanted to leave the table. They just sat there, crying. Somehow it seemed okay to do that.

Life will go on for sure. They had managed without him and they will manage very well without him, but for now... it was his physical presence that they missed so deeply. It was love in its purest form.

Days passed by... Seasons changed. Autumn gave way to winter and winter to spring.

Tharani stood at the foot of the long flight of steps and looked up at the temple right at the top. She could see the unrelenting blue sky above, with the Sun beating down. Could she do it? Did she have the strength? Did she have what it took to get to the top?

This was her penance. Tharani, the extremely religious woman, believed in penances and prayers. So what was she praying for this time? She was praying for the well-being of her girls—that they live a happy life, that they get married and have children. She was praying for her dream of having grandchildren to come true. Love is a powerful motivating force and so is posterity.

She took the first step, then the next, and soon she was on her way. She sat down and rested for a while at the landings of each flight of steps before moving on. There was no hurry. She had practiced climbing up and down stairs at home just to be able to do this, and it helped her now. Soon she was almost at the top. She could see the trees clearly now, the people moving in and out of the temple, circling the temple and ringing the bell. She could hear the chants.

She took a deep breath and climbed up the last flight of steps. And then, she was at the top! She had done it!

Tharani's heart was racing. She moved to the railing. The steps were cut out from a rock on the hillside itself. It was amazing how well it was done considering how old the temple was. It had been built centuries ago when there were no machines. It had all been manually chiselled out. The railings on either side were made out of the rock too and were broad. They doubled up as seats for weary travellers to rest on before moving on. There were monkeys everywhere. You could hear their screams as they moved around. Most of them were tame and harmless except for the fact that they could take off with the belongings if one wasn't careful. The best way to treat them was to leave some bananas and snacks on the railings for them to pick up. But never feed them by hand because, then, they followed you around expecting some more where that came from.

Tharani sat there till her heartbeat normalized. She then looked down the steps. Had she really climbed up all those? Wow!! She felt a sense of accomplishment and pride. "I still have strength," she thought, "And while I am strong... ." she turned the other way and looked at the temple, "while I am strong, you, my God, must help me settle my girls."

She got up and climbed up the short distance to the temple. This part, although a very short distance indeed, was somehow harder. There were no steps, just a gradual slope that led to the temple.

She was breathless again when she reached the temple and had to stand there for a while. She could hear the ringing of the bell as the priest did the puja. She could see the worshippers outside, standing with folded hands. The chants... some more ringing. The priest came out with a plate in which camphor had been lit. He waved the fire in the direction of the worshippers on all sides of the railing, and then he went in. Some more ringing...

Tharani waited for the puja to finish, then she went into the cool interior of the temple. The moment her feet touched the cool marble, she felt a sense of peace descend on her. It was always like this. She was closer to her God; she was home.

She went up to the railing. The priest came out and she gave him her offerings of flowers, fruits, coconuts, etc., and said, "For the well-being of my daughters." But the priest did not take her offerings. She looked at him, confused and repeated, "Please take the offerings. It is for the well-being of my daughters."

He smiled and gave it back to her and went in. She turned. Yamini and Sitara were standing there and smiling at her. "What are you doing here?" asked Tharani, "And how did you come up?"

"By bus," grinned Sitara, "We can't climb steps and all. We're too old and I have arthritis."

Yamini was smiling at her mother, "We saw you leaving and followed you."

"Where is Sheila?"

Yamini pointed to a place further down where a few steps had been cut from the rock. It was surrounded by trees and very cool and shady. Sheila was there. She had placed some food for the monkeys and was talking to them.

Tharani sighed. She smiled at her elder daughters, "What do you want?"

"We want you to sit and talk to us before you say all these prayers."

"There's nothing to say. I'm just praying for your well-being."

"You're praying for us to get married you blackguard!" said Sitara, dramatically, "You should be shot dead."

"So what? I'm just praying."

"Oh my God!" exclaimed Sitara, even more dramatically, putting a hand to her forehead, "Just praying!! Where is your faith woman?"

Yamini burst out laughing, and even Tharani was smiling. "Get out of my way girls. Go back home. I left home to escape from you all and you've come here too. The monkeys are better than you."

"I can see that," said Sitara, pointing to a couple of monkeys. They were sitting on the railing and one monkey was taking out tics from the other monkey's fur, "You can take them home."

"What do you want?" Tharani demanded.

Yamini went up to her mother, "Come," she said, leading her towards the shady place, "We will sit and talk."

"Okay," said Tharani, docilely, allowing herself to be led.

Yamini led her there, then let go of her arm. Tharani sat down on the landing, her feet on the steps below.

Yamini and Sitara sat down to the left of her, on the railing. Sheila, who had turned to see them come, now abandoned the monkeys and sat down at her mother's feet.

"Well?" said Tharani.

Yamini took her hand and placed it between hers, "We understand that you want what's best for us. But there are somethings that we want too... our wishes. We want you to respect these wishes."

She saw that Tharani was listening to her intently, and she continued, "You... .you know that we girls... especially Sitara and I... .we are different from the girls our age. You know that. We have seen things, experienced some things, and now, we're in a place in our lives where we have always wanted to be. We are happy, we are at peace. Nobody has bombed our house, no one has... you know. We earn well, the right way! We enjoy life. We love coming home, to see your face, thinking, "What did she cook for us today?" Thinking how was Sitara's day? Did Sheila pass her exams? I rush home feeling happy. For the first time in my life...and in Sitara's life... Let it be this way. Please allow it to be this way. This... this climbing up the ladder all the time! Getting married, facing discrimination, having our past hauled up against us, having to prove that we are good women. Enough Mamma! We just want to be with you. We don't want all these things. Please let us be!"

Tharani's eyes filled with tears, but she kept quiet. She took the pallo of her sari and cried into that. Sitara placed an arm on Yamini's shoulder, but Yamini was firm. She sat there waiting for her mother to come to.

Eventually, she looked up and at Sitara. "Do you also feel the same way?"

"Oh yes!" said Sitara, promptly. "You're just finding ways to get rid of me. If I go, who will wipe their hands on your sari pullo? Who will give you sudden hugs? Who will share all your very personal stuff with you? Who will eat from your plate? Ah? Tell me!"

There was complete silence after this speech as Tharani stared at her daughter, wide-eyed. Then she asked slowly, "Am I to say 'thank you'?"

"I think so! The least you can be is grateful."

Yamini's lips quivered and her eyes were full of merriment.

Tharani said doubtfully, "Thank you?"

"You can do better than that!! It will do for now. Keep practising."

Tharani looked at Yamini and they both burst out laughing. Sitara grinned, then started to giggle, which turned to full-blown laughter. Sheila was laughing too.

They all laughed and laughed. Finally, Tharani wiped the tears from her face and blew her nose.

"Well, if that's the way you girls feel, I have nothing left to say. I can't force you into marriage."

"Yey!" Yamini and Sitara did a hi-five.

"I will never have grandkids."

"Oooohh!! So that was your plan all along. We're just some sacrificial goats so that you can have grandkids."

"I'm not saying…"

"You just did!"

"Ah, well, everyone dreams of holding their grandkids and buying them toys and spoiling them rotten."

"Sheila will do the needful."

"What!" said Sheila, shocked, "What did you just say?"

"Well," explained Sitara, "It's the right thing to do. Step up girl! Be a hero. Have three kids, one for each of us, and dump them all on Mummy and get going."

"Do I look like a baby-making machine to you?"

Sitara reached out and patted Sheila's stomach. "Nice stomach. Big... accommodative..."

Sheila squealed and moved away from her hands. "Stop it! Mummy, stop her!"

Tharani reached out and spanked Sitara on the arm.

"Ouch!" said Sitara, "That hurt!"

"It was meant to."

"You're mean!"

But she reached out and flung herself on her mother. The hug sent them both spiralling backwards on the landing.

Tharani screamed, "Sitara! Get off me! Please! Yamini, don't just sit there! Do something! Help!"

Passers-by smiled at the scene.

Sitara got off her mother and sat down. Tharani got up too and glared at her. "You do that once more, I'll... ."

"I'm hungry," Sitara said, changing the topic abruptly, the way only she could.

"Me too!"

"Me too!"

Tharani sighed, "Then let's go have breakfast in some hotel."

"Malli Idli Shop," said Yamini, "They have the best idlis."

They all nodded.

"And their idli podi is just yum!" said Sitara.

"You girls are sure you don't want to get married?"

"Ma!!"

Author's Bio-Data

Glory Sasikala is a poet, novelist, and publisher currently residing in Chennai, Tamilnadu, India. She was born in Kolkata and did her schooling there. Her husband died in a tragic road accident in 2008. Glory has two children, Tennyson and Rimona, daughter-in-law, Hannah, and a very cute grandson named Samuel. Glory had been working as language editor and quality analyst but has now transitioned to full-time writing, especially novels. Writing remains her passion. Her poems have been published extensively. Her first novel, 'Goodbye Papa' was published by Prof. P. Lal, Writers Workshop, Kolkata. She is also the editor and publisher of the online poetry and prose magazine, 'GloMag,' published every month on Facebook, featuring writers from all over the world. She brings out two hard copy versions of the magazine every year.